Head
GAMES

Head GAMES

a novel by

keri mikulski

razOr
bill

Head Games

RAZORBILL

Published by the Penguin Group
Penguin Young Readers Group
345 Hudson Street, New York, New York 10014, U.S.A.
Penguin Group (USA) Inc., 375 Hudson Street, New York, New York 10014, U.S.A.
Penguin Group (Canada), 90 Eglinton Avenue East, Suite 700, Toronto, Ontario, Canada M4P
2Y3 (a division of Pearson Penguin Canada Inc.)
Penguin Books Ltd, 80 Strand, London WC2R 0RL, England
Penguin Ireland, 25 St Stephen's Green, Dublin 2, Ireland (a division of Penguin Books Ltd)
Penguin Group (Australia), 250 Camberwell Road, Camberwell, Victoria 3124, Australia (a
division of Pearson Australia Group Pty Ltd)
Penguin Books India Pvt Ltd, 11 Community Centre, Panchsheel Park, New Delhi – 110 017,
India
Penguin Group (NZ), 67 Apollo Drive, Mairangi Bay, Auckland 1311, New Zealand (a
division of Pearson New Zealand Ltd)
Penguin Books (South Africa) (Pty) Ltd, 24 Sturdee Avenue, Rosebank, Johannesburg 2196,
South Africa

Penguin Books Ltd, Registered Offices: 80 Strand, London WC2R 0RL, England

10 9 8 7 6 5 4 3 2 1

ISBN: 978-159514-387-7

Copyright 2011 © PrettyTOUGH Sports, LLC
Series created by Jane Schonberger
All rights reserved

Library of Congress Cataloging-in-Publication Data is available

Printed in the United States of America

This book is dedicated to every girl who has dared to dream, especially the original Pretty Tough girls, Alex and Maddie, and the newest Pretty Tough girl, Kaci Olivia. You are all such an inspiration.

one

Nothing "Monday morning story worthy" ever happens to me. Excitement is saved for the gorgeous girls at Beachwood Academy. You know the ones who, even when they're not looking for it, find fun in the most peculiar places. Like shopping: "Can you believe that super hot movie star I ran into at the mall asked me to lunch?" Or while walking the dog: "I know it was so random. This guy pulled up next to me in his BMW. And next thing I know, I'm backstage at *his* concert." Gripping an orange ball inside the paint is about as exciting as it gets for me.

But then, bright and early one Saturday morning, everything changed, and my life instantly became story worthy.

After completing my usual Saturday morning routine (Breakfast? Check. *Beachwood Sun* sports section? Check. Obsessively thinking about our big game against Richland? Check. Dreaming of being in the WNBA? Check.), I throw my thick brown hair into a messy ponytail and take off toward the wooden boardwalk trail that ends at my fave California coast basketball court, only a few yards from the crashing aquamarine waves. The worn wooden path is completely and utterly deserted except for a couple early morning joggers. If I'm lucky today, I'll spot some serious eye candy. Just as I'm thinking this, my cell phone buzzes.

FR: BANANA:
CALL ME ASAP!!!!!!!!

I quickly text back my BFF Hannah Montgomery AKA "Banana":

TO: BANANA:
FREAKING ABOUT FASHION SHOW AGAIN?

Staring at my reflection in the phone, I run my fingers under my brown eyes to erase the leftover mascara marks from one of Banana's makeovers. (She says mascara is a must for my wide-set eyes). Then I go online and leave a good morning post on fellow freshman Chloe's wall. Chloe's so sweet to post on my wall this morning, even though she's been out with the flu.

FR: BANANA:
YES! MEET ME @ CAF. ASAP.

Hannah hearts her ASAPs. I shove my phone inside my royal blue Beachwood Academy basketball bag and break into a jog. I hate to be late. Plus, Coach makes us run suicides for every second we're tardy. Not fun.

The trail veers off at the recreation complex, an elaborate facility that houses a skate park, basketball and volleyball courts, a gym—complete with full-size Olympic pool—and a sauna, among other exciting features. (Well, exciting for people like me who are totally obsessed with sports.) When I reach the end of the path, I look up. And there he is: Zachary Michael Murphy. Just like he has been for the past six mornings in a row. Only this time he's alone. The court lights, still on from the night before, shine on him, as he successfully makes jump shot after jump shot. Leave it to him to never be too far from the spotlight.

Zachary Murphy. My future boyfriend (I wish) and the only guy in the entire high school who checks off on my boyfriend must-have—height. And he happens to be nice, way older (he started kindergarten a year late—plus, he's a junior), athletic, and hot, too. I swear I'm not shallow. (He's not the most popular guy at school. Christopher Phillips is.) And it's not like I've had a boyfriend, or even a kiss before, to actually understand must-haves. But I know what I need. Because, let's face it, I'm kind of walking around with a serious boyfriend handicap: my height.

I'm not just tall. I'm mega tall. Six feet. Seventy-two and three-quarter inches. And my doctor says I'm not even done growing yet. I'm taller than everyone at Beachwood Academy except exactly nine male teachers, three coaches, the principal, the E-wing janitor, and one student—and fourteen others with future height *potential* (because of their ginormous feet).

This explains my other nicknames over the years: Towering Taylor Thomas, Giraffe, Horse, Elephant, and another one about my anatomy, but I prefer not to think about that one right now.

"Hey," Zach says, smiling and balancing a bright orange basketball on his hip. Yum.

"Hey." The words barely make it across my lips because (a) this is Zach, and he has never said "hi" to me before (well, except for after an AAU game when a bunch of my friends went over to his house to hang out with his sister Zoe—but that doesn't even really count because he was saying "hi" to the whole group of us). And (b) I can't breathe because according to Zach's status (which I've recently begun reading religiously), my height-appropriate soul-mate is at long last single.

Last week, after I finally mustered up enough courage to friend-request Zach (mainly so I could stare at his page and possibly drag some pics of him onto my desktop), I logged onto my account and was shocked to discover that he had friend-requested me first. *Me.* Naturally, I rubbed my eyes (not once but three times) and logged off and then on again because I assumed I must have accidentally signed onto Hannah's account or something. Of course, when I finally realized that I had read his request correctly, I accepted it in less than seven seconds. Since then, I've been checking (not stalking, I swear) Zach's page daily. Okay, and sometimes even hourly from my phone depending on how much time I have on my hands.

But last night at exactly ten twenty-seven, something happened. His relationship status changed from "in a relationship with Kylie Collins" to single. Yes, S-I-N-G-L-E.

"Want to play?" Zach asks. Before I can answer, he sets up and shoots.

Swish.

I look up at the sky for a second, wondering if his now-ex-girlfriend is hovering above us in an aircraft. For a second, I picture Kylie Collins hanging out of an army helicopter with an AK-47 in hand, ready to light me up.

He bounce-passes the basketball to me. My instincts take over, and I feel for the familiar seams, set up, and shoot.

When the ball plunges through the net, I meet Zach's chocolate eyes and spot his teeny eye-sprinkles. See, if you get close enough, Zach's acorn eyes have tiny amber speckles. I did. Get close enough. Once. It happened exactly two weeks ago. While running between my first and second period classes, I stumbled and accidentally slammed into Zach, launching him four steps back and spilling the contents of my pale blue Nike bag all over the floor. It was like a bad slow-mo action scene. But, being the super sweet guy he is, Zach stopped and squatted immediately, gathering my stuff. But, what did he pick up? Not the pack of Extra Polar Ice gum or the tube of L'Occitane lip balm my mom forces me to carry around. No. Instead, he seized my annual handmade bedazzled birthday card to my aunt. Don't ask. It's a tradition. And not a tradition I *ever* wanted Zach to find out about.

Interrupting my eye-sprinkle-related daydream, Zach retrieves the ball and bounce-passes it to me. Just then, I catch the court lights refracting off the very same eye-sprinkles I'd been thinking about. Perfect. Meanwhile, the ball continues to bounce and bounce until it rolls onto the sand.

I allow myself another moment to fully take Zach in. He's wearing his Beachwood basketball fleece with jeans pulled low on his hips. Just low enough, in fact, that when he lifts up his arms to shoot, his fleece inches up to show off the tan smooth cuts of his lower back muscles. Yum. He runs his fingers through his dark hair, and I feel a wave of heat rush through my body.

"Uh. You don't have to play if you don't want to." He grins.

I look down at my practice clothes—vintage gray cotton shorts with the word *Basketball* written across my butt, a birthday present from my aunt two summers ago. Yup. The butt shorts. The ones that don't exactly do wonders for my pale legs.

Why? Why did I wear these shorts today? Of all days . . . Oh, that's right. They were my only clean shorts because Mom has been M.I.A. lately (meaning no wash), and I figured a Saturday practice meant zero chance of a Zach sighting. (According to last night's status, Zach was out late last night surfing with Nick.) And even if by the slightest chance I did see Zach, I figured that there was no way he was going to look at me, let alone my butt.

See, this is against all social rules. Zachary Murphy doesn't hang out alone with girls like me. I mean, since I started shooting baskets here first thing in the morning in the beginning of September, Zach hasn't even noticed me. He hangs out with tiny girls like Kylie, Chloe, and Missy. That's just the way things work at Beachwood. Once in a while, guys like Zach will maybe talk to me, or text me, or even message me. But most of the time, I'm like a chess piece to strategically place in line in order to snag Hannah or another cute girl I happen to hang out with—girls who hold their heads up high and proudly stick their butts out when they wear gray shorts with words written across their cheeks, instead of feeling like total poseurs.

This was no easy lesson to learn. At first, I believed my family, doctor, and even Hannah when they told me that my height was a good thing and would actually attract guys. So, last year, I decided to try to be like everyone else my age and spend seven minutes "in heaven" with Dylan Davis inside Hannah's downstairs walk-in closet during her fourteenth birthday party.

After ensuring that the closet door was firmly shut (no need for P.D.A.), I bent my knees and partially squatted to match Dylan's five-feet-five-inch frame. Then I shut my eyes and gently parted my lips just like I watched Leighton Meester do on *Gossip Girl*. My breath catching in my throat, I waited for his lips to press against mine. And . . . nothing. A few seconds later, I heard a deep sigh and opened my eyes to witness Dylan's white knuckles wrap around the doorknob, the light of his open cell phone reflected off his face as he counted down the seconds.

"Uh. Sorry. Just tell everyone we hooked up or something. You're just way too big."

Lesson learned—height is great for hanging off a basketball rim. Not so great for hanging with guys.

Zach jogs over to retrieve the ball off the beach.

"One-on-one?" he asks, picking up the ball and looking up.

I nod. My heart seriously melts like an M&M left in someone's hand for too long.

"Read about you in the paper today. Another twenty-twenty, huh?"

"Yup." I smile as I always do when someone compliments my basketball skills. I'm used to the basketball compliments. They're normal and easy . . . unlike my social life.

Zach glances at my braces-free teeth (two months ago this Thursday—yay!) and I wonder whether I have a poppy seed wedged in there from the everything bagel I ate earlier. Turning my back toward him, I pretend to stare out at the ocean as I dig my nail in between my two front teeth to check for any strays.

"Your ball. Make it, take it," he says, grinning and passing the ball to me.

Zach stands in front of me with his hands up, giving off the most scrumptious scent ever—a combination of mint, musk, surf, and sand. We're nose to nose. So close, I can smell his peppermint breath.

I dribble for a bit, cutting and maneuvering toward the basket. Zach slides behind me, one hand up against the small of my back and the other high in the air. I move my feet, jockeying for position. At the same time, my heart picks up speed.

I lean in, shove, and hook the ball toward the hoop. Zach extends and jumps, attempting to block my shot, but he's too late. The ball effortlessly sails through the net.

"Nice," he says, grabbing the ball. He bounce passes it back to me. "Two–nothing."

I walk over to my duffel and pull out my cell to see how I'm doing on time. Thirty minutes until basketball practice. Quickly, I do the math in my head and figure I have about ten minutes left in beach-court paradise.

"Going somewhere?" Zach asks, placing his hand on his hip.

"Practice." I dribble the ball back to mid court. "But, I'm not done beating you yet."

"You're not getting by me that easily again," he says, squatting in a defensive slide position.

"Wanna bet?" I answer. Basketball is the only thing that makes me feel invincible. When I'm out on the court, I say and do things that I never would otherwise in a bazillion years. Like, after I sink a perfect three, I sometimes wanna pull a *Titanic*-style Leonardo DiCaprio maneuver and run across the gym yelling, "I'm king of the world!" (or I guess, in my case, *queen*). And although I'd never have the courage to actually do that in real life, sometimes I wonder if anyone would really notice. (If it wasn't game time, that is.)

I look at the basket and figure that I could probably get by him at the baseline, but then I remember: this is Zach I'm dealing with. I've seen his moves, and he's not exactly the type of player who will just let me past. Although I'm ashamed to admit it, the reason I'm so in tune with Zach's style of play is because "seeing his moves" is really an understatement. Not only have I watched him run, jump, and pivot in the flesh, but—since our cyber friendship began—I've been known to view a few (or twenty) of the game highlights he regularly posts online. In fact, it's sort of become one of my favorite secret pastimes.

I drive hard toward the basket, but Zach steps in front of me and I lose my footing, causing me to crash down, knobby knees first, on the pavement. The ball soars through the air and rolls onto the sand. Again. Luckily, my outstretched hands break my fall. But, with all the momentum, one of my pasty knees drags on the pavement like a tire screeching to a stop.

And it stings. Real bad. Like the time I fell ice-skating at Hannah's fifth birthday party and needed fifteen stitches.

I'm screwed. Not only because next Friday is the game against Richland, the biggest game of my life—coaches from an elite Amateur Athletic Union summer team, the (AAU) SoCal Suns, will be coming to evaluate my playing ability against Richland's stud center in order to determine whether to offer either of us a spot—but also because playoffs are right around the corner, along with our chance at a three-peat, a third championship in a row. And of course, I'm going to have to play injured. Great.

"Are you okay?" Zach asks, staring at me, as if I'm some sort of freak show. After a few very uncomfortable seconds of silence—which feel more like ten hours—Zach offers me his hand.

"I'm fine," I say, through clenched teeth. I gingerly stand up on my own and assess the damage. Sure enough, bright red blood is streaming down my shin.

"Do you want me to call someone?" Zach pulls out his cell phone, ready to dial nine-one-one.

"Seriously, I'm good." I smile tightly through gritted teeth.

Zach follows me as I limp toward the silver bleachers to grab my duffel.

"Thanks for the game," I squeak as I toss my bag over my shoulder and hobble toward the beach, desperately hoping that he hasn't caught just how much warm, crimson liquid is currently rolling down my leg.

"Yeah. See ya," Zach says. I give him a kind of nod-slash-grimace in response and turn away as another swell of pain washes over me. With each movement, the stinging increases, but I do my best to minimize any visible signs of agony in case Zach is still looking. Sixteen excruciating steps later, I hear the dribble of the ball in the distance.

two

Having now survived the second most humiliating moment of my life (the first was during a "pay what you weigh" dinner when my parents chose to hand over a buck and some major change instead of nickels and dimes like everyone else's 'rents), I decide that even though the walk from the complex to Beachwood is a mere three blocks, I should take the time to clean up the blood still streaming down my shin. After unzipping my duffel, I pull out an extra sock and wipe away the blood, promptly turning my sock red. Then I pour some water on the sock and use it to dab the gash. Ouch.

The walk to Beachwood feels longer than ever before. My mind swirls with thoughts of Richland and their star center Nikki Rodriguez. And I'm about to lose it when I finally arrive at my high school, Beachwood Academy—B-Dub. Opting for the entrance closest to the gym, I push the door open to our brand new eco-friendly building (a recent donation from an ultra-successful alum, and one of the various interconnected structures that make up the high school portion of the campus).

As I hold the door open for my teammate Eva (who has dyed her hair more times this season than I've earned twenty-twenty games), Matt Moore barrels by me and scales the steps. He sails through the air and lands feet first on the freshly cleaned linoleum below (all signs point to Beachwood's having an army of little elves who operate by the principle: "No speck of elite private school dust shall ever go un-mopped").

"Hey, there's my favorite English partner," he says, straightening up. He looks at me with his deep brown eyes and seeing my slight limp, an expression of concern flashes across his face. "You injure yourself before practice even starts?"

"Yeah. It doesn't hurt too bad anymore. And besides, we can't all be immune to injury," I tease him, loving the way his signature hoodie hugs his neck. Today it's another gray one with *Beachwood Lacrosse* written across the front in white block letters. "You also here for practice?"

"Just getting in an early morning warm-up before I have to head home." He runs his hand over his black buzz cut.

"So you actually have time to work out? You know, with all the partying and hooking up you do?" I joke. And honestly, who knows how much of that is right on the money? Matt transferred to Beachwood from Beverly Hills High earlier this year, and his background is a complete mystery (which means that it's also prime fodder for the rumor mill). Given that the majority of my classmates started out together at Beachwood Middle, any new blood is a source of serious interest. And with the way that Matt doesn't talk about his past, curiosity has only grown larger over time.

Sometimes I find myself wondering whether he's hiding something—a terrible, dark secret or a crazy mistake. Other times, I just think that he likes to keep the speculation and rumors circulating. Not that that's hard to do—ultra-competitive private school students have no difficulty concocting elaborate stories in seconds. (Our SAT writing scores are second in the state.) Naturally, every girl at school wants to be added to his supposed list of conquests. Except me, of course. He's too short. And besides, if there's any truth to the gossip, I don't want anyone's sloppy seconds. Or thirds. Or fourths, for that matter. Well, except for Zach's. And he's a one-girl-at-a-time kind of guy. (At least I hope so.)

Matt grins, showing off two deep dimples. "Taylor Thomas finally came up with a funny." He takes a few steps backward and checks his watch. His face turns grim. "Gotta go. Dad's waiting. See you in English." Matt turns around and sprints across the lawn.

I hold the door for two more cheerleaders and then walk into our gym, bracing myself for our star junior guard Kylie's inevitable hysterics. As always, I take in the multiple royal blue Wildcat championship banners that adorn the walls. Then I glance up at my dad's framed number four jersey, challenging myself to play to the best of my ability. Although basketball has always come easy to me (I get it from my dad who was a tremendous talent—hence, the hanging jersey), I am constantly pushing myself to reach the next level of play, especially because it's my fault that Dad never got to go pro.

Not surprisingly, my self-directed pep talk is soon interrupted by the sounds of Kylie being comforted by her BFF Missy. Like Kylie, our star guard, Missy is a platinum blonde (Hannah insists that neither of them were born that way) and a fellow junior.

I guess Kylie heard about Zach's recent status update. And from the looks of it, the decision was not mutual. With only a week to prepare for the Richland game, the last thing we need is for one of our best players to be having a complete meltdown. Unfortunately, if the last time Kylie and Zach had relationship trouble is any indication, then our team is in for a rude awakening.

Kylie used to be far less intense, back when she and I actually hung out together after AAU basketball games. Before she began dying her hair and having it blown out in perfect, Blake Lively–looking waves. Before she and Missy became BFFs. And before she had a fist-to-cuffs brawl with Natasha Morris, the Beachwood junior class president, right in the middle of B-Dub's newly paved parking lot, simply because Natasha— who had never previously stepped foot in the gym—suddenly started being the loudest member of Zach's cheering section. Kylie never got over it. She always thought that Zach must have been secretly cheating on her with Natasha. And ever since then, Kylie has been completely obsessed with catching him in the act, so much so that she's officially become a permanent resident of crazy-town.

I keep my eyes cast down and walk toward the ball rack. Not that I did anything wrong. Zach just wanted to play some one-on-one. Most likely, he's just setting me up to improve his basketball skills or to eventually chat all things Hannah or Chloe or Missy or Jessica or someone way hotter and smaller than me.

And anyway, Kylie has a completely different reaction when it comes to me. So, it's not likely that she's suddenly going to start perceiving me as a threat. Once she totally caught me gazing at Zach during Beachwood's annual holiday charity drive, and she couldn't have cared less. In Kylie's eyes, I'm a total zero.

I grab a ball, walk past fellow freshmen Abby and Zoe practicing foul shots, and shoot outside the three-point line at the side net. Sure enough, Kylie's violent sobs are still audible.

"Hey, girlie. Thanks for helping me out with my math homework last night." Jessica, a sophomore forward, greets me at the basket. She drives toward the net for a layup. Then, she catches the ball and turns around, never breaking the conversation. "Did you hear about Kylie and Zach?"

"What happened?" I ask, pretending not to know. Out of the corner of my eye, I sneak a peek at Kylie and discover that she's busy slamming a basketball against the concrete gym wall. Not good.

"Last night over dinner at Missy's house, Zach told Kylie

that he's into someone else." Jessica's long, black ponytail sways as she sets up and shoots at the foul line.

"Really?" I exclaim, surprised to discover that the break-up may have been due to more than just Zach's disgust with his crazy girlfriend. Oops, that was harsh. My injury must be getting to me. Time to regroup and think nice.

Standing underneath the basket, I check my knee. It's scabbed over, but still screaming.

"Yup." She moves closer toward me, and I get ready for the inevitable: "Zach's really into Hannah, etc . . ."

Like the time during seventh grade, when I was crushing on Michael Trono. I was still super naïve about the height thing and thought for sure Michael was going to be my first kiss. And for three weeks, Michael hung out with me. All the time. We even shot baskets together just like Zach and I did today. Actually, I did all the shooting. Michael kind of sucked. The whole time I swore he was going to ask me to Beachwood Middle School's annual Holly Ball. Sure enough, two weeks before the dance, Michael walked up to my locker and said, "Hey, can you . . ."

Cutting him off, I fluttered my eyelashes and bellowed a big *yes*, beaming.

"Thanks. I really appreciate your help. Message me to let me know if Hannah says yes."

Second lesson learned. Everyone likes Hannah. Not me.

"And get this," Jessica whispers in my ear. "I heard that after he left Missy's house, he called you hot."

My stomach does a three-sixty. No one has *ever* called me "hot" before. Except maybe my mom when I'm sick.

"Does Kylie know?" I squeak.

Before Jessica can answer, Coach Jackson blows the whistle, signaling the team to huddle up. Jessica and I race back over (well, she races—I do a weird jog-slash-hop thing) and take our seats on the bleachers.

Even though I'm worried about how Kylie's latest meltdown is going to impact the team, and more importantly, even though my stomach is still swirling over the hot comment, I'm excited to hear what Coach has to say about our plan for dealing with Richmond.

"Okay, Wildcats," Coach begins. "There's something serious I need to talk to you about." Tucking her Beachwood gray T-shirt into her blue mesh shorts, Coach scans the stands.

Joy. Coach heard the Zach and Kylie news. Ever since Kylie's suspension (yup, due to her fight with Natasha), Coach keeps an eye on the Beachwood social scene. Now, whenever she hears about drama, she quotes some Henry guy who hung out in the woods for a while and says, "Success comes to those too busy to be looking for it." In other words, if we're too busy playing basketball to make drama, we're bound to succeed.

That's when we see Martie, athletic-director-slash-English-teacher-slash-girls'-soccer-coach-extraordinaire, enter the gym. Carrying a clipboard in her hands, she jogs on over to our little circle. She and Coach Jackson give each other a slight nod, and then Coach turns back to us, resuming her speech.

"Most of you know Martie for one of the many hats she wears at this school. And we're very fortunate that even with all that she has going on, she has graciously agreed to fill a vacancy that just opened up here in girls' basketball."

Looking around, I see that the other members of the team have also begun shifting uncomfortably and casting furtive glances out of the corners of their eyes. It's clear that they're all thinking the same thing as me: *What the heck is she talking about?*

Continuing, Coach Jackson catches us completely off guard with her next announcement. "I have some bad news. Coach Bennington has had to take a leave of absence."

What? What's wrong with Coach B? Is she sick? Did something happen?

"Is she okay?" Tamika, our captain, asks, nervously twirling a thin braid.

"Yes. Coach B is fine. She just has some personal things she needs to take care of and has requested some time off."

Martie pipes up. "So, Coach Jackson is going to take over as head coach, and I'm going to work with you as your assistant."

Again, we all exchange puzzled looks.

Martie's life is like an episode of my mom's old TV series, *L.A. High*. Rumor has it that Martie grew up in Crenshaw, attended Beachwood years ago, and played for the U.S. national soccer team after graduation. Then, while she was away playing in the World Cup, her sister was killed in a drunk-driving accident. Now, as the first female athletic director at B-Dub, she's a big success story. *But . . .* despite her many accomplishments, the fact is she has absolutely *no* basketball experience.

"No offense," Tamika pauses. "I know you're this amazing soccer coach and everything, but what do you know about basketball?" She crosses her arms.

Martie smiles gently. "I'm in the process of studying your plays, and Coach Jackson is doing a fabulous job of preparing me." She hugs the clipboard to her chest. "Plus, I have some team-building activities up my sleeve that have proven to be very effective. If we learn to play as a team, we'll win as a team. Teamwork transcends all sports."

Team-building activities? This isn't gym class. We need to prep for our game against Richland on Friday, the one where the SoCal Suns summer club coaches will be peppering the stands. The same game that if we win, we're golden to earn our three-peat—for only the second time in Beachwood's elite basketball dynasty's history. And no Coach Bennington? Coach B is the Pat Summit of Southern California. She's the primary reason I decided to attend Beachwood. I've been dreaming of playing for her ever since my dad took me to a B-Dub championship game when I was in second grade.

Ignoring the team's frustrations, Coach Jackson continues. "If you are all willing to give this new dynamic a chance, I'm completely confident that we can continue playing as well as we would have under Coach B. With me focusing on the more technical aspects of the game and Martie concentrating on the mental part, we're stacked. Martie is a phenomenal team builder and a pro at teaching mental toughness." Coach pauses briefly, and—I could be wrong—but I think I see her eyes flick over to Kylie. "And um . . . those are aspects of our game that could certainly use a little help."

Tamika lets out a deep breath (guess she doesn't think that's too terrible of an explanation). At almost exactly the same time, Kylie emits a shrill gasp. Only I don't think it has anything to do with what Coach just told us. Nope, she's gasping because of the shape that just whipped across the gym toward the men's locker room. Zachary Michael Murphy. And I'm pretty sure that he just winked at me.

three

We're going over our baseline play for the zillionth time when it happens.

"Hey, Zach, there she is." Hoots and catcalls echo from the direction of the boys' locker room.

I survey the court, my eyes landing on Kylie. Although she's supposed to be watching the court while waiting her turn to take over the guard position, her eyes are glued on Zach. With the type of death stare she's giving him, I wouldn't be surprised if her eyes started shooting laser beams.

"So, did you have to stand on a dune to kiss her or what?" I hear Nick say.

I freeze. Kiss? What is he talking about? And standing on a dune? I'm definitely the tallest girl here by five inches. I'm the only one that a guy would have to climb a dune to reach. Kylie switches her glare to me. I'm frozen like Rodriguez when I drive past her toward the basket.

"Taylor? Are you listening?" Coach Jackson shouts, tucking the basketball under her arm.

"Yeah, sorry." I jog to my spot, which for me means standing under the net with my hands up. Sometimes this is all I have to do to sink ten baskets a game. See, I'm not only the tallest girl at Beachwood; I'm also the tallest girl in the entire conference.

After I jog to my position and raise my hands, I feel beads of sweat forming on my forehead and on the back of my neck. Tamika passes me the ball. I bank it off the backboard into the basket.

Kylie steps onto the court to take her turn. With a scowl plastered across her pale pink glossed lips, she launches the ball at me as hard as she can. It snaps into my palm. I turn toward the basket and finish my layup. My heart hammers inside my chest and a droplet of sweat rolls down my back.

If Kylie's looks could kill, I would be one dead—wait a sec. Make that *Jessica* (who is standing directly in front of me) would be one dead forward.

"Jessica, how could you? You're my teammate! You and me in the locker room after practice." Kylie points and glares at Jessica.

Jessica turns around and shrugs her shoulders at me like she does during tutoring when she can't figure out a formula.

I pick up the ball and toss it back to Kylie whose tense face flips faster than a cheerleader at halftime. She grins sweetly at me.

Of course Kylie couldn't possibly think Nick was talking about Towering Taylor Thomas. And honestly, I'm not quite sure either. I mean, Jessica *is* five feet eight.

four

Fr: Banana

Where r u?????? Major news about fashion show!!!

I wonder what could possibly be going on with the show that Hannah would want my help with. It's not like I know anything about style or fashion design. Nope, that's definitely her department.

I toss my duffel bag over my shoulder and hightail it out of the locker room before I witness the unsheathing of Kylie's claws. (I mean, I know I can take her one-on-one, but what spews out of her mouth is way worse than any fist fight). With Jessica trailing on my toes, she must be thinking the same thing.

Poor Jessica. At the end of practice, Kylie looked flustered, red, and definitely ready for battle, kind of like the time she caught Amanda Maisley helping Zach study for his history final after school. Yes, just studying. The next day during lunch, after Amanda stood up to chat with Missy (not realizing, of course, that Missy was in on one of Kylie's schemes), Kylie deviously left a packet of ketchup on her seat. When Amanda returned, she sat down and . . . *splat*. Amanda was sent home three hours later after a teacher finally informed her she was walking around oblivious to a big, red splotch *right there*.

But what tipped off Kylie's craziness and set all-time psychotic records was the infamous Chloe Simpson incident. It's supposedly the only "proven" Zach cheat. But I don't believe it ever happened. Chloe's such a nice person; she's always messaging me and has been helping Hannah out with the fashion show. Anyway, rumors swirled around Beachwood that Chloe kissed Zach at Surfrider Beach while Kylie was away skiing in Telluride over Winter Break. A week later, someone hacked into Chloe's page and sent embarrassing wall posts to all her friends divulging their biggest secrets for the world to see. Seriously humiliating stuff. Poor Chloe spent the entire month of January trying to clear everything up. Just when things were looking up for her again, the hacker hit her Twitter account, sending tweets about some made-up deep dark secrets. She shut her accounts down and hasn't been the same since. You just don't mess with Kylie and her crew.

"You okay?" I ask, walking alongside Jessica toward the caf.

"No worries," she says. She finger-straightens her ebony hair. "Everything will get worked out eventually. But, you might want to stay clear of Zach for now. I mean, eventually, Kylie's going to find out he likes you."

"Maybe he likes you," I say, holding the door to the side lawn open for Jessica. "Kylie seems to think so."

"Come on, Taylor." Jessica walks across one of the *Welcome to Beachwood Academy* rubber mats and halts at the doorway. "He's totally crushing on *you*. Nick said he had to stand on the dunes."

"Yeah, but you're five-eight," I point out.

"Seriously, Taylor? Zach needed to stand on the dunes to reach someone who's five-eight? Really? They had to have been talking about you."

My stomach does another flip and I shrug. "I guess."

"Hey, do you mind if I Skype you tomorrow to go over geometry before Monday's test?" Jessica asks, changing the subject. "Proofs and I aren't exactly best friends right now."

"Haha. Sure. I owe you one." I smile.

"Thanks." Jessica slips out the door and sprints across the grass.

Realizing that I'm running late to meet Hannah, I scurry down the massive hallway and briskly cross the interior courtyard to the cafeteria. Upon pushing the heavy double doors open, I'm immediately taken aback by the overwhelming number of newly installed sewing machines, spools of unraveled measuring tape, and piles of discarded fabric. And then there's the usual abundance of royal blue and white Wildcat banners hanging from the walls. Another reminder of the legacy our team has to live up to.

"Tay! Finally!" Hannah screams from the far side of the

caf. As she sprints toward me, I notice that the look on her face is somewhere between stressed and insanely excited. Oops—I really should have texted her back.

"I was convinced you were going to ditch me after practice," Hannah groans. Hannah's oblivious to how lucky she is: She's petite and perfect, about five feet four inches tall, and blessed with wavy but not curly pale blond hair. Plus, she always exudes a real sense of confidence. As opposed to me. In fact, she manages to mix punk and vintage styles with her own designs and look really amazing . . . which is probably why everyone at Beachwood *loves* her.

Today, for instance, she's dressed in an oversized black Volcom tee with rolled-up jeans that she's stripped and re-sewn with a series of fabric swatches (probably stolen from her sister's dresses). Around her neck is a chunky necklace made out of bottle caps, fabric flowers, and mini Care Bears dolls left over from her childhood. And last but not least, she's sporting a pair of gray Vans that she's embellished with jewels from 1920s dresses purchased at a thrift shop.

Hannah and I have been best friends since the second grade. When I brought my favorite Bratz doll, named after Lisa Leslie, to show-and-tell, Hannah was so impressed with the mini-basketball jersey I'd made for her and the intricate backstory I'd concocted that she begged me to come over and play with her after school. After an afternoon of Bratz bonding, we pinky swore best friendship forever.

"What's up?" I ask, swinging my duffel bag over one of

the royal blue ergonomic plastic chairs and plopping myself down on the chair next to her.

"Okay, don't freak," Hannah begins hesitantly.

Uh-oh. *Whatever Hannah has to tell me, please don't let it make today any worse than it is already.*

"All right. I'm just gonna say it." Hannah takes a deep breath, and then, releasing it, quickly blurts out the big news. "I signed you up for the fashion show."

"Wait . . . *what*?!?" My palms clam up and my heart starts pounding so loudly, it feels as if it might almost burst.

"You're going to be my model!" Hannah grins, showing off her perfectly straight, white teeth.

"Are you serious?" I shriek. "A model? ME?"

"I knew you would have this reaction." She grabs my arm and drags me toward the mad throng of girls measuring, pinning, and sewing. "But, you're gorgeous and tall. And I need someone to wear my designs. And uh, Chloe was going to do it, but you know, she has the flu and is out for the rest of the month. So, you're it. Thanks so much for helping me out. You're going to have a blast!"

For a few seconds, I'm so paralyzed by fear that I can hardly breathe. I scan the room once more and my suspicions are again confirmed. I'm completely out of my element. Unlike the girls around me, who are each dressed to the nines, with their perfectly coifed hair and their designer duds, I'm once again clothed for comfort. I wonder what percentage of them is secretly laughing to themselves about "the giraffe with the duffel bag" who has no business being here.

Seeing the deer-in-the-headlights look on my face, Hannah realizes that she's going to have to keep me focused if she doesn't want me to freak. She stands me in front of the wall and pulls out her digital camera.

"Smile!"

For a second, my eyes are blinded by the flash, and I'm almost able to forget exactly what I'm doing here. Then Hannah ushers me next to her and turns the camera around so that she and I can both see the screen. When the image appears, Hannah literally folds over, cracking up uncontrollably. "Seriously? Are you going to a funeral?"

"Banana, I can't do this. And anyway, I'm super busy. The Richland game, which the SoCal Suns scout will be at, and our chance to three-peat are both coming up. And there's also this drama that we need to talk about."

"Oooh! Well, you know I love me some drama. But for now, just smile."

I half grin this time. Hannah snaps the pic.

"The fashion show will help boost your confidence, which will make you so much better prepared for your big games!" she says, glancing at the pic with a content expression on her face. After motioning for me to remove my warm-up jacket, she pulls out a tape measure from her bag. "Now, stand still while I take your measurements."

As Hannah wraps the tape measure around my waist, hips,

and other parts of my body I never wanted measured, let alone in front of the Beachwood elite, I shift around awkwardly. Meanwhile, Missy walks by with Brooke Lauder (another member of Kylie's crew and fellow junior), who, judging by the fat sketchbook in her hands, is also participating in the fashion show. Just my luck. They freeze in front of me like they spotted a fifty-percent-off handbag sale at Prada, eye me up and down, and then show-whisper to each other.

"Taylor, what are *you* doing here?" Missy asks, grinning at Brooke and dosing her lips with expensive-looking gloss.

"Duh." Hannah replies indignantly. "She's a model."

"Seriously?" Both girls look me over once more, giggle, and continue walking.

"Banana, I'll do your homework for you. Beat up your sister. Anything. But *please*"—I hand Hannah her tape measure and place my hands in the prayer position—"convince Jessica to take my place."

Hannah moves my arms out like a scarecrow as she measures my (lack of) chest. Looking up at me, she winks. "You're going to be fabulous."

But what does Hannah know? When she's in a closet with a boy, he's not checking his cell phone.

five

After Hannah finishes taking my measurements, I decide that if I play around on my phone for the duration of this nightmare, people might not notice that "Big Bird" (another one of my unfortunate nicknames) got lost on the way to visit Bert and Ernie. And mistakenly walked into a room populated by an entirely different species.

My stomach flutters as I stare at my phone. Wow. A comment on my "Going to practice" status. I just recently got up enough courage to begin posting status updates. Hannah and her sister Violet text updates every five minutes, as does almost every student at my school, but this week is the first time I'm posting about my life for the world to see. Normally, I'm all about blending. And when it comes to, "Hey, this is what I'm doing," I'm usually completely cyber-shy.

Turns out it's Chloe who posted. Her message says, "Thanks for the flair. Have fun at practice!"

"You're welcome," I begin to reply back. Then a flush creeps up my back; that's definitely not a good enough response to someone who took the time to comment even though She's sick. I delete and type, "You're welcome and feel better soon ☺" Then, I feed my puppy and send a February heart back to my Aunt Denise (she sent me one twenty minutes ago). Next, I add a couple more friends to my heart list and reply to some posts. (I always reply to as many as possible—I mean, it totally makes my day to receive replies, so why wouldn't I want to make someone else's?) Finally, I update my status with a "With Hannah at fashion show rehearsal." As soon as I see my new status typed out on-screen, I delete it. Too much.

"What happened to your knee?" Hannah squishes her nose like the time she bit into a raspberry-crème filled chocolate truffle. Hannah hates raspberry.

I shove my phone back in my duffel and look down at my scab. My Zach scab. Now that it's stopped hurting, I've realized that it isn't bad enough to mess with my season. So, it's kind of become a souvenir of sorts. "I was on the beach court and . . ."

"Okay, everyone." Mrs. Sealer, the fashion club advisor, sharply claps her hands. "All models please make your way to the Mark Chase Auditorium for rehearsal in fifteen minutes."

"This is it." Hannah lets out a deep breath and shifts into *Project Runway* mode. "After you're done with rehearsal, you're coming over my house. Since your measurements are different from Chloe's, I have a ton of work to do."

"You know, we can go to your house now . . ." I offer, wondering how I'm going to get through a rehearsal for something I know nothing about.

Hannah's blue eyes bulge. "You totally have to go to rehearsal! You have to practice your walk." She spins me around so that I'm facing a group of teeny-tiny girls taking turns strutting their stuff in the corner of the cafeteria. Each one seems to radiate more attitude than the next, and I'm mystified by the way that they make walking a few steps look so animalistic, as if they are about to pounce on their unsuspecting prey.

"See," Hannah says, recognizing the look of awe on my face.

At the same time, Hannah's sister Violet, clad in a navy blue, almost toga-like mini dress, glides past me, with her Beachwood entourage following close behind. Although the girls seem to be carbon copies of each other—each has perfectly straightened hair (which Hannah insists is the result of Keratin treatments, not genetics), luminescent, bronzed skin (thank you, sunless tanning), and towering stilettos that make their calves look they've been sculpted from marble—from the way that the other girls trail behind her in V formation (yes, I'm serious), it's clear that Violet is the ring leader.

As the girls are about to leave the caf to make their way to the adjacent auditorium, Hannah calls out, "Hi, Vi! Guess what? Taylor's filling in for Chloe at the last minute. I'm sooo relieved."

Stopping for a second as one of her minions opens the door, Violet gives Hannah a little wave (more like a flick of her wrist) and then winks at us as she prances out of the cafeteria.

Hannah turns to me and shrugs. Meanwhile, I collapse on the nearest chair. "I can't, Banana. I don't belong here."

She rolls her eyes. "When are you going to accept the fact you're Selena Gomez's twin? And anyway, I need you. Pllllleeeeaaasseee . . ."

I give her a blank stare.

"Come on, you know you can't say no to me."

Letting out a deep breath, I admit to myself that she's right. She has been my best friend for years, after all. "Fine," I say.

Hannah's mouth bursts into a huge grin, and she does a little jump (for all her "alternativeness," she's a girly-girl at heart). "Yay! You're the best. I promise we'll have your fave vodka sauce at my house tonight."

She leans toward me. "Soooo, tell me what this drama is all about. . . ."

"Well, uh . . . Zach changed his status to single last night and Kylie has lost her mind, and I think she may be under the impression that I did something with him. Or maybe Jessica. I'm not sure. But anyway, she's really angry, and I'm worried about the team. And you know how I've been crushing on Zach since kindergarten. . . ."

"That's perfect! I didn't want to tell you right away, but Zoe told me yesterday that Zach thinks you're hot!" She flashes me another huge smile. "You must be completely freaking out."

My stomach turns inside out. That's two of my friends who heard that rumor. (Or three if you include Zoe—who should know. She's Zach's sister after all.) See, Oprah is right.

All this "paying it forward" and being nice is finally working. "Kind of . . ." I say.

"Kind of!" Hannah screeches. "So what are you going to do? Are you going to text him? Hook up? Meet him at the beach courts tonight for a little . . ." She winks. "One-on-one?"

I feel my face flush. "We already did that."

Hannah stands up. "WHAT?!? You hooked up with Zach and didn't tell me!"

"Shhh! NO." I look around and spot Missy standing like a scarecrow as she's being measured by Brooke. From the way that they seem to be calmly engrossed in conversation, I gather that they didn't hear anything. "No, we just played basketball."

Hannah's eyes widen.

"Listen, I don't want this getting out."

Hannah flips her long bangs away from her cobalt blue eyes. "Seriously, Taylor, when are you going to stop worrying about everyone else and go for it? I mean, you're such a beast on the court."

"I don't care what people think." I place my hands on my hips.

"Sure. You keep telling yourself that." Grabbing me by the shoulders, she looks at me intently. "Now come on, Mrs. Murphy. Go be a beast on the B-Dub runway."

And with that, she shoves me toward the auditorium. Inside the catwalk looms. *Is it too late to make a run for it?*

six

"Okay, ladies." Mrs. Sealer stands at the edge of the catwalk in front of us, roster in hand, her black eyes surveying this year's crop of models with obvious disdain. "Please line up according to height. Tall girls in the back."

I slowly stand up and wait for the other girls to take their places in line. I'm definitely in the back. In fact, I don't think I've ever not been. Every pic, every family shot, every class portrait: same story.

"Vi." Mrs. Sealer points to Violet. "Since you're the veteran of the group, you'll go first." Giving the girl next to her an "awww, me?" look, Vi sashays to the front of the line.

As Violet takes her first steps onto the catwalk, everyone stops to stare. Even Mrs. Sealer beams. With a recurring bit part on a CW show and the confidence of Mischa Barton pre–career tank, Hannah's tiny, platinum blonde older sister has an "it factor" that makes even the faculty at Beachwood go gaga.

While watching Vi troll the catwalk, I can feel my hands starting to shake. I *so* don't belong here. This is even worse than the time my mom signed me up for acting classes with

Tom, her acting coach. What a disaster. After two lessons, and more line flubbing than I care to remember, a tomato-red Tom told my mom acting just wasn't for me and that it would be an offense to the art form to continue as my instructor.

Mrs. Sealer signals for the members of Vi's entourage to each take their turns and then summons Missy, who is followed by Brooke and a gaggle of girls I've never met. Seemingly dismayed by some (if not all) of the performances, Mrs. Sealer glances down at her list and calls out, "Chloe Simpson!" When no one responds, she looks up and repeats "Chloe Simpson! Where is Miss Simpson?"

"On her knees?" I hear Brooke cackle.

"Um ..." I step out from behind the heavy royal blue curtain that was shielding me. (That's the beauty of the Mark Chase Auditorium—it seems as though it's permanently set up for a runway show, hence the draping curtains that hang on either side of the rear of the catwalk.) "I'm here to take Chloe's place. She's sick."

"Oh ..." Mrs. Sealer looks me up and down, raising one eyebrow. I've always wondered how someone does that. I try it with my own eyebrow, but it twitches instead. "And you are?"

"Taylor. Taylor Thomas."

"She plays basketball," Allison Webb, a senior and Violet minion, says in between snorts of giggles.

By this time, my knees are about to buckle.

"Okay, Taylor. You'll be last."

I file in back and cross my fingers that this torture will end soon.

Interrupting the procession of girls attempting to navigate the runway, Mrs. Sealer sharply claps her hands for attention. (Apparently, she thinks this is the way that fashion gurus are supposed to behave.) "Now, this is what's going to happen on the day of the show. The club music will be pumping and you will walk to the end of the catwalk and back, just like Vi did today."

Violet and Mrs. Sealer look at each other, approvingly, as if they are each privy to a secret that no one else knows and that they do not care to share.

"It's simple!" Vi exclaims, as if putting oneself on display is the most natural thing in the world.

"Yes, it absolutely is," Mrs. Sealer replies. "Now, everyone, place your hands on your hips and let's practice loosening up our cores."

Mrs. Sealer presses play on the drama club's stereo and the sounds of Lady Gaga belting "Rah-rah-ah-ah-ah-ah! Roma-roma-mamaa!" pump from the speakers. Vi, Missy, and the rest sway and jut their hips. Some girls even close their eyes.

"That's it girls. Get a feel for your hips. Visualize your inner tiger." Mrs. Sealer joins the action and actually roars a couple of times.

I stand stiff and watch the rest of the girls move their hips like they're Beyoncé or something. I'll walk the catwalk for my BFF, but there's no way I can jiggle my hips like that.

"Taylor, join us please. Most of these girls have runway experience. You're a beginner and really need to practice. Now, sway."

I lift my arms and place them on my waist. Then, I slowly move my hips from side to side. But, instead of looking like Beyoncé, I resemble my grandma doing the hokey pokey at a family wedding.

"No. No. No." Mrs. Sealer walks toward me. She places her hands on my hips. The rest of the group stops gyrating and gathers around us. "This way." She rocks my hips back and forth with me like we're dancing. "That's it."

Oh my god. This is humiliating.

Mrs. Sealer lets go of my hips. "Okay. Now that you've all got that down, time for those of you who last practiced your struts in flats and for those of you who didn't get turns"— pausing for a second, Mrs. Sealer looks me in the eye—"to try your hands at doing your runway walk in heels."

Upon doing a little jump (guess the prospect of subjecting us to more agony is too exciting to contain), Mrs. Sealer shuts the stereo off and pulls out a pair of tiny, sparkly, silver spiked heels from a box. They're serious Cinderella shoes. "Taylor, you first."

Think happy thoughts. Think Zach. Think Zach changing his status to "in a relationship with Taylor Thomas." I walk toward Mrs. Sealer like I'm about to walk the plank.

After I attempt to shove my size-ten flippers into the size-seven heels to no avail, my evil fashion stepmother, Mrs.

Sealer, takes over, using all her one hundred pounds to push until my toes crackle and crunch like Rice Krispies in milk.

"I don't think they fit, Mrs. Sealer." Missy chuckles, darting her eyes from me to her buzzing iPhone.

"You're right, Missy." Mrs. Sealer halts and wipes the sweat off her brow. "Taylor just needs so much work on her walk. I really wanted her to wear the heels."

"I have an idea," Vi declares. "How about Taylor just walks on her tippy-toes?" Turning to me, she says, "Tay-Tay, you'd be okay with that, right?"

My chest tightens.

"I really don't have to go first," I plead.

"Believe me, you need all the help you can get," Mrs. Sealer adds. "Now relax."

Snorts and giggles erupt behind me. Mrs. Sealer presses play on the stereo and Beyoncé's "Single Ladies" fills the auditorium.

I lift myself up, so that I'm standing on the balls of my feet as if I'm doing a calf exercise, and walk gingerly down the runway.

"Sashay. Sashay. Bring out your inner lioness. Your inner vixen. Come on, Teri."

"Taylor," I say.

More giggles and snorts.

I stop at the end of the runway and turn around.

"This is an important moment. This is when the flash bulbs go off!" Mrs. Sealer excoriates. "So jut your hip. Strike a pose. Be a cougar." She stops herself and looks around nervously. "I mean, a tiger."

Even more giggles and cackles. I guess the rumors about her and the varsity quarterback, Chris Olay, were true.

I resume my walk back to the rear of the catwalk, when Mrs. Sealer shouts, "Practice! Practice! Practice! You need more practice!"

I walk back on my tippy-toes, nearly losing my balance as I attempt to sway my hips. When I finally reach the seats, I come down off my toes and quickly locate a spot far away from everyone else.

Hannah owes me big time.

seven

"How'd it go?" Hannah asks, as I plop down in the cafeteria chair next to her, which just happens to be the only seat in a five-chair radius not covered by sewing supplies.

For a moment, I pause to appreciate having made it out of the auditorium, and then it all comes rushing out. "I stink. I don't belong anywhere near the freaking runway."

"Oh, don't say that! I'm sure you were great."

"If by 'great' you mean that I'm never going to 'own the catwalk' or 'be a tiger,' then yup, I was awesome."

Hannah chuckles. "Don't be so hard on yourself! It was your first time practicing. Think about girls like Vi who do this kind of stuff all the time. And imagine what those girls would be like on the basketball court."

At the mention of Violet's name, I can feel the anxiety begin to creep over me again. "I just need to get out of here," I say.

Not one for negativity, Hannah bounces out of her chair and announces, "Well, I did promise you some vodka sauce."

Hearing the words "vodka sauce," the storm cloud overhead immediately begins to lift.

During our walk to Hannah's house, I spill the deets about my run-in with Zach on the basketball court.

When I'm finished, Hannah lets out a deep breath. "This just gets juicier and juicier. Let's look at the facts. Zach changes his status. Then you guys play one-on-one together. Then he winks at you, even though he knows Kylie is watching. Plus, he told his sister that he thinks you're hot. And get this . . ."

"What?"

"You should really be sitting down for this one. . . ."

"What is it????" I ask, unable to contain my excitement.

"He told Nick about you! That totally means he's into you. If a guy tells his friends about you, then he wants to hook up with you." She jumps up on the concrete curb, pretending she's on her skateboard. Hannah's been a skateboarding fiend ever since she watched Lyn-Z–Adams Hawkins on the X-games two years ago. Naturally, this particular obsession really freaks her parents out. Fashion design, they can understand. Skateboarding, not so much.

"So, what happened after you fell? Don't leave me hanging!" Hannah may actually be more excited about this whole Zach thing than I am. "Did he scoop you up like a newlywed and slam his lips on yours?"

"Uh. No."

Head
GAMES

"Oh Tay, that blows.... You know, not because that means anything at this point, but because . . . you know. . . ."

Hannah is the only one at Beachwood who knows I've never been kissed. I'm beyond ashamed to tell anyone else. I mean, Hannah has kissed three guys already, including one boyfriend. (In other words: major make out time). That's three different kissing styles to try out. And I'm way behind.

I shake my head.

Hannah takes a deep, dramatic breath. "Maybe, he wants it to be special."

I shrug. "I don't know.... Maybe I don't even *really* like Zach." Even as I say the words, I know they're not true. Of course I like Zach. I might even be in *love* with Zach. But . . . I *hate* drama. Especially the Kylie kind. And besides, Zach's so out of my league.

She rolls her eyes. "Are you going to be one of those girls who likes guys, but then when they like you back, you're over them? No offense, but you'll never ever kiss anyone that way. And if you worry about what everyone else thinks, you'll end up living all by yourself, with nine hundred cats for company. Just like my Great Aunt Sally."

I swallow a lump in my throat. "*Sooo* . . . don't laugh, but is your Great Aunt Sally tall???"

eight

When we turn the corner to Hannah's street, my eyes are immediately drawn to her house. Sometimes I forget just how big Hannah's digs are. You could spend an entire week inside and not realize Hannah's family was there with you.

After Hannah types in the security code at the gate, we walk up the winding driveway and scale the marble steps to the chiseled-glass front door. I drop my duffel in the foyer, catch a glimpse of the killer ocean views through the wall of picture windows that line the rear of the house, and follow Hannah up the curving staircase toward her room.

Hannah's room is my second home. In fact, her mom even added another bed in there just for me. A cute pale blue canopy bed identical to the ones that Hannah and Violet have slept in from the time they were in kindergarten. But, four years ago, when Hannah decided to punkify her room, she sawed off her own canopy, painted the ivory posts black, added a purple comforter, and threw on patchwork pillows she sewed herself, using scraps of material from vintage dresses. She then ripped up her cute pink-and-white bedspread (supposedly so that she could use pieces of it in her designs when she's trying to be "ironic") and shoved the canopy décor in her closet never to be seen again.

But no canopy complaints from me. I'm just happy that slumber parties at her house don't involve sleeping bags. Otherwise, I'd probably end up slathering my entire body in Bengay before attempting any drives toward the basket.

The instant we walk into her room, Hannah and I each fall onto our respective beds. As I'm just about to close my eyes (I shouldn't be tired, but today was an especially crazy day), I hear a "tschhh" sound. Looking over at Hannah, I see that she's started violently tearing out pages from a magazine.

"Whoa. Way to take out your frustration on something that can't talk back," I say, completely confused by what's going on.

"Not frustrated," Hannah answers. "Just really need to get cracking on your garments for the show." Stopping for a second in the middle of her magazine-shredding frenzy, Hannah looks down. "Oooh, wait. This is perfect!"

She folds the page into an airplane and tosses it to me. I catch the page easily, unfold it, and am shocked to see what all the fuss is about. In my hand is a photo of a model dressed in a barely-there mini. *What the???*

"What do you think?" Hannah asks.

"Huh?"

"For the show. What do you think of wearing something

like that for the fashion show? Of course, I'll have to alternify it. But something along those lines . . ."

"Do you really think I can pull off this look?" I ask. The model in the photo is rail-thin. I wouldn't last a minute on the court if I were that tiny.

Hannah grabs the pic back. "Of course you can. You're my inspiration."

"Can you really make it in my size?" I crinkle my nose and hug my legs to my chest.

For a second, I feel a twinge of pain from bending my busted-up knee. Then, a horrible scenario flashes in my mind. What if Hannah spends all this time working on my outfit and it rips? Or worse, what if I walk the runway and I trip? AKA exactly what happened on the basketball court this morning.

"Of course. You'll look fab." She grabs a textbook from underneath her bed, lays the page out flat, and begins drawing on the pic. I guess this is what she means by "alternify."

Meanwhile, as she's working, I meander over to her computer. Sitting down at her desk, I prop my feet up and open her MacBook. Time to check in on the latest Beachwood gossip.

"Voila!" Hannah says, sitting up. "My masterpiece is complete."

While I'm typing in her password, Hannah's bronzed mother, Celia, peeks in. "Hey, Taylor." She smiles, showing off her super-shiny bleached white teeth. I grin back and gently close Hannah's computer. I mean, it's one thing if Hannah knows I'm checking up on Zach, but it's another if her mom does.

"Are you staying for dinner, Taylor?" asks Ceila, clutching a copy of the *Beachwood Sun*.

"I promised Tay her favorite," Hannah responds, impishly grinning at me.

"Penne vodka sounds perfect tonight! I'll tell Jacques." Tripping over Hannah's bedazzled, army-green skateboard, Celia shakes her head. "How's basketball?"

"Great," I say, leaving out the fact that our win/loss record depends on Kylie's love life, that we lost our head coach today, and that the biggest club scout in all of Los Angeles told my dad she'll be at our game next Friday. Call me crazy, but I assume that a woman who spends her time painting the ocean and perusing boutiques doesn't care about hearing how my whole basketball career is on the line.

"Do you think you guys are going to win the division this year?" She sits down on Hannah's plum couch in front of the window.

"Yup," I say and then pause. "Well, I hope so."

"I'm sure you guys will do great. We all remember your being named MVP twice in middle school." She delicately crosses her legs and looks over at Hannah. "Hannah was so proud of you. She could hardly stop talking about how well you did."

I glance over at Hannah to telepathically communicate

how worried I am about living up to my reputation as a basketball all-star, but she appears to have become engrossed in the magazine on her lap and is busy folding and unfolding the corner of a page.

Oblivious to whatever's going on with Hannah, Celia continues. "So what's on the agenda tonight? Beach? Boys?" She giggles, absentmindedly swinging her dainty foot.

"Mom," Hannah says, looking up from the photo in front of her and dramatically rolling her eyes.

"I get the hint." Celia stands up, pinching Hannah's cheeks on the way out. "I know you girls always think you're too cool to tell your mothers the dirt."

"Whatever," Hannah says, rolling her eyes once more just in case her mom missed out on the full effect the first time around.

Celia gently clicks the door shut behind her. A second later, Hannah hops on her skateboard and rolls across the beige carpet. (Hannah may be creative, but it's difficult to punkify carpeting.) "Perfect," she says, taking off toward her door.

I open Hannah's laptop again and sign in. I type Zach's name into the search box. Relationship status is still single. *Yes!* For further confirmation, I click onto Kylie's page and scroll down. And then I see it. Her relationship status is also single. Since she and Zach first started dating, Kylie's *never* been listed as single. Not once. Not even during the many times that the two of them broke up. This must be the real deal. My stomach flutters. *Maybe Hannah is right. . . .*

Hannah returns from her design room with a piece of apricot fabric and skateboards across the carpet toward me. "So, what's up tonight?" she asks, looking over my shoulder.

I click back to my home page and scroll through the updates. "Jessica's hanging out at the beach courts. And so are Nick and Missy."

"Awesome." Hannah skateboards over to her bed, grabs her phone out of her bag, and furiously types. Her status pops up on the computer screen in front of me with the words *Skate Park tonight*. So *that's* what she has in mind. The skate park and the beach courts are right next to each other at the rec center. Instantly five comments appear. Hannah tosses her phone back in her bag. Unlike me, she never worries about replying.

Having accomplished my recon mission, I'm about to log off when something catches my attention. I rub my eyes. It can't be. Zachary Murphy—*the* Zachary Murphy—just wrote on my wall.

I stare at the words. *Hey, how's your knee?*

nine

Violet's high-pitched voice interrupts my wall-post bliss. "Han, where are my Prada clutch and my Versace cream silk top?" She stomps toward her younger sister's closet, throws the double doors open, and begins tossing articles of clothing behind her.

"I don't have your stuff, Vi." Hannah jumps, attempting a trick on her skateboard. "And if I did, I would have already stripped it."

Hannah may love her sister, but she doesn't have any patience for what she calls "Vi's theatrics." But that doesn't seem to matter to Violet. She knows she can have any guy she wants. *Whenever* she wants.

As Violet continues to fling items out of Hannah's closet, Hannah flips her board up and catches it. Turning her attention toward me, she says, "I love it when boarders do that. You know, flip their boards at the top of the half pipe and then catch them? You know what I'm talking about? Tony Hawk does it all the time."

"Yeah, uh . . . Banana," I reply, unsure how to respond

without giving my best friend license to land herself in the hospital. "Tony Hawk has his own video game empire."

"Where. Are. They?" Violet's normally, perfectly toned skin is beet red when she looks up from the mountain of clothes she's created.

"I told you I don't have your stuff. Geez."

Violet's phone screeches The Black Eyed Peas' latest. "Urgh . . ." she says, before pulling her iPhone out of the back pocket of her jeans. Then, she looks at the text. Immediately, her face relaxes.

"Who's that?" Hannah looks over Vi's petite shoulder.

"No one," Violet answers, quickly texting back before shoving the phone in her pocket.

"Aren't you running out of Beachwood guys by now?"

Violet ignores Hannah.

Turning to me, Hannah's eyes light up. "So what do *you* want to wear tonight?" Hannah hearts dressing me.

I shrug my shoulders, playing with the keys on Hannah's MacBook.

"I would *love* to dress you, Tay-Tay!" Violet offers, eyeing me up and down. "I mean, you totally need a makeover. And I have so many ideas. To begin with, you'd look AH-mazing in skinny jeans. Not many people can pull off skinny jeans and red heels, but I bet you can." She picks up a silk, red tank top from Hannah's pile of clothes and holds it up just below my face. "And red is definitely your best color. It brings out your pale complexion, dark eyes, and brunette hair."

"You think?" I crinkle my nose. It's hard to avoid being pulled into the swirling winds of Tornado Violet.

"Totally." The Black Eyed Peas plays again and Violet grabs the phone from her pocket, a smile crossing her face as she sees who the text is from. Looking up, she remembers her reason for being here. "I swear to god, Hannah. If I find out you destroyed my clutch and dress like you did my Chloe top last week, you're so dead." She points at Hannah.

"Whatever," Hannah rolls her eyes. "Who is it this week? Dylan?"

"Nope." Violet winks and runs her thumb across her phone. "It's Matt Moore tonight. He's such a sweetie."

I almost puke. It can't be. I know there are rumors about him. *But* . . . he's different. (At least around me.) And *so* not Violet's type. I mean, I hadn't thought so . . .

Giving us a little Miss America–wave good-bye, Violet sashays out of the room and slams the door behind her.

"I probably should stop tearing up her clothes for fabric. But she's such a brat." Hannah giggles. Then she stares at the open computer screen. "What's that?"

"Nothing." I close the laptop.

She shoves next to me and opens it. Her mouth falls open. "Wait, Zach left you a post, and you didn't tell me?"

As I'm about to inform her that I just noticed it when Vi interrupted us, Hannah seizes the opportunity to quickly type "Why don't you come over and kiss it?" under "How's your knee?" Before I can swat her hand away, she presses enter.

That did not just happen. My heart beats wildly and I can't swallow. "What are you doing?" I try to push Hannah out of the way. But for a tiny girl, she's freakishly strong, and I can't budge her.

"You have to show Zach how you feel." She giggles.

"This is not funny. He's dating one of my teammates. If Kylie sees that comment, she'll kill me."

"Correction: He *was* dating one of your teammates. He's single now, remember?"

I use my hips like I would to box out an opposing player and catapult Hannah a couple of steps to the side, managing to gain back control of the laptop.

Except that's when I realize I'm too late. There's nothing I can do. The comment is already out there for all of Beachwood—and the world—to see. It's official. Game over.

Swish.

ten

The most amazing sound ever. The only thing that can distract me from the fact that it took five whole minutes for me to figure out how to delete Hannah's comment. Five long minutes during which Zach and Kylie and the rest of Beachwood (okay, my cyber-friends, but still) could see just how desperate kiss-less Taylor really is for a guy's attention on a Saturday night. Or at least that's what they'll think.

My sweet sound is interrupted by a smack.

"Foul," Nick barks at Kylie, attempting a steal with hacks and skin-slapping.

"You're up eighteen to twelve. Stop crying. Loser," Kylie counters, breathless.

That's when I see what's got Kylie stressed. (Not that it's hard to do.) *He* came. To the beach court. Zachary Murphy. I'm stunned that he and Kylie would be willing to hang out together, but I guess that's one of the many weird things about their relationship. No matter how many times they're "on a break," they still hang out. If you ask me, Kylie's a glutton for punishment.

Having said his hellos to the members of the girls' and boys' b-ball teams who came out tonight, Zach runs onto the court. Play begins, and soon enough I feel his warm hand nudging the small of my back for position.

Zach leans in closer. If he were just any opposing player (especially my rival Rodriguez), I'd throw him off and get into better defensive position. But this is Zach. And he's touching my back. And I can feel his breath on my neck. And I don't want it to end.

Play continues around me, and Nick passes to Chris who alley-oops the ball to Zach, who, moving away from me, fakes right, steps left, and hooks the ball into the net. Zach tumbles into me as he lands and catches my forearm. My heart pounds. "Sorry," he says before dashing down the court to play defense.

I jog by Kylie, who is shooting Zach a look that would freeze fire, and set up underneath our net. Zach slides behind me, again placing one hand against the small of my back and the other in front of my face. My heart picks up speed.

Kylie dribbles across half-court, attempting to outmaneuver Nick, who sticks close behind. She steps around Nick and fires the ball to Missy.

Missy breaks toward the basket and immediately bounce-passes the ball to me, inside the lane. *It's on me.*

Zach moves closer.

I freeze.

Matt Connelly, another senior, slaps the ball out of my hands and takes off toward his basket.

"What the heck, Taylor?" Kylie shouts my way.

My chest tightens. Even at a Saturday night pick up game, nothing but the best is accepted at B-Dub. "Sorry, I don't know what happened."

"Whatever." Kylie snatches the ball from Matt and launches it at Zach. The ball ricochets off his foot and rolls onto the sand. He looks at her, bemused, and turns to Nick, shrugging.

A squeak escapes Kylie's lips. Then she takes control of the situation, declaring, "I'm parched. And it's time for a water break anyway."

I mosey over toward Hannah, who's just finished practicing her ollies at the adjoining skate park.

"Did you catch all that?" I ask.

"Yeah, I could barely concentrate on my skating with all the sexual tension going on over there. Zach's totally been checking you out," she says.

I look down at my Nike shorts and pull my baby blue fleece sleeves over my hands.

"In fact, I think he's looking at you right now."

"Banana, will you cut it out? He's not staring at—"

"Hey."

I turn around and there's Zach, jogging toward me, his dark brown hair tumbling onto his forehead in soft waves.

Mouthing "told ya so," Hannah beams at me and skateboards away in the direction of her boarding buddies.

The second she leaves, I take a breath, preparing myself for the inevitable "So, Taylor, you know how you and Hannah are so close . . ." followed by a rambling explanation of how much he likes her. And how I, as her best friend, am in the unique position to help out.

Except, this time the rambling explanation doesn't come.

Instead, he grabs my hands and pulls me onto the sand beside him. Our bodies tumble to the ground together, and my stomach drops. "You're really good at basketball," Zach says.

"Wait. What?" I ask, dumbfounded.

"You're really good. I've never played against a girl as good as you."

"You've probably never played against a girl as tall as me before."

"I've seen you on the court. You're good." Zach looks up and moves his hair out of his eyes.

He's watched me play? I stare at the sand, tracing the shape of tiny basketballs with my index finger. Then I remember I'm supposed to respond. "Thanks," I muster, my tongue sticking to the top of my mouth like glue.

Then, Zach does something that I never in a million, bazillion years would think he'd ever do. He slides down toward my feet, looks up at me with his make-me-melt eyes, leans down toward my scraped knee, and kisses (yes, kisses) the Band-Aid. "Does that feel better?"

My heart stops. He read Hannah's comment. Maybe she does know what she's doing after all. I nod, unable to recall how normal people are supposed to behave in these situations. But all I can think is, *Zach kissed me*! (Well, my knee anyway.)

Then, silence. Weird, uncomfortable silence. *One Mississippi, two Mississippi, three Mississippi . . .*

"Hey, Taylor." *Uh-oh*, that voice. I know that voice. I turn around. Sure enough, Kylie has come to ruin my moment.

Turning to Zach, she announces, "We need to talk," and, grabbing his hand, pulls him to his feet. She then flips her golden hair over her shoulder and says, "See you at practice, Taylor."

"Bye," Zach adds, following Kylie. And then—the icing on the cake—he winks at me.

Just like that, the two of them take off, and it dawns on me: What's worse than Kylie completely freaking out because I'm hanging out alone with her boyfriend? *No reaction.* Nada. Nothing. Like I'm absolutely no threat to her whatsoever. Like I'm Zach's sister or cousin or something.

I push myself off the ground and stand up. And then I remember. Zachary Michael Murphy kissed me. Beat that, Aunt Sally.

Instead of trekking back to the court, I attempt to avoid all signs of Beachwood Academy by taking the bike path home.

"Where are you going?" My heart skips a beat. Matt Moore, still wearing his adorable hoodie, sits on a small sand hill, a few feet away from a group of Beachwood girls, including an impatient Vi, who's busy texting and rolling her eyes.

"Oh my gosh, you scared me!"

"Well, I guess you scare easily." Matt grins.

"I thought you were a murderer or something."

"Maybe I am," Matt replies, his smile getting even bigger. "So, where are you going?"

"Home." I pull out my iPhone to check the time. Three texts from Dad—one checking in on me, another, reminding me of my ten o'clock curfew, and a third, reiterating that this is the last time I'll be allowed to go to the beach with my friends if I don't text him back immediately to let him know I'm okay.

Matt tosses a red cup on the sand and grabs my hand. "I hate you for making me want you so much."

"Dude, love the Edward Cullen quote, but I think you have the wrong person," I laugh and quickly snap my hand back. I text my dad back, letting him know that I'm on my way. The last thing I need is for him to worry. Then I glance back at Vi, who's still pacing around on her phone, probably making the uber-important nightly club decision. I widen my eyes as I catch sight of Vi pressing what looks like the "End" call button on her phone.

"Why don't I walk you home?" He walks down the dune.

"I'm good.... And anyway, I don't feel safe being accompanied by a vampire." I try to crack a smile, but I'm starting to feel slightly woozy again.

"Fill me in on Murph on Monday." Matt smirks. "I saw you guys on the beach."

"And fill me in on all the partying you do this weekend," I add, giggling.

"Come on, Matt," Vi says, walking back over toward the group.

He shrugs and jogs over to her, giving one final look in my direction. I'm surprised to see that the two of them look so cute together. They're just about the same size.

Steadying myself as I resume my journey home, it occurs to me: Hannah's with her new skateboard gang. Zach's with Kylie. Matt's with Violet. And Taylor Thomas is walking home with a kissed boo-boo.

eleven

Fifteen minutes later, I scale the steep driveway toward my front door, taking a moment to think future-WNBA-player thoughts as I stretch my long legs before heading inside. Then I text Hannah and deep breathe like I learned at the Sun Salutation Yoga class my mom dragged me to this summer. (Tell my mom you feel stressed sometimes, and she'll have you yoga-ing it up before you can say "downward dog.")

I open the door to find my dad, still dressed in his collared shirt and khakis from a round of golf this morning, sitting in his favorite recliner in front of the flat screen TV in the great room. "Is Mom home?" I ask, hoping that she's around to hash out the details of the fashion show with me.

"She's asleep," my dad says, mindlessly playing around with the golf club on his lap. My dad plays a lot of golf. I guess it's a diversion. So he can forget about his glory days as a star guard at Beachwood and UCLA, and his two seasons playing professionally in Europe. *Before my being born ruined his dreams of making it to the big time . . .*

He places the club to the side of the chair.

"So, Spider, did you have fun with your friends?" Urgh. The infamous spider nickname. At least it's been shortened from the original "Daddy Long Legs." (Get it? Really long legs? Dad says I've had them since birth.)

"Yup." I take two steps at a time. Dad's been trying hard lately to "connect" about something other than basketball. I think our basketball relationship works just fine.

"Did you run today?"

"Yup." I stop mid staircase.

"Did you shoot and practice left-handed layups?"

"Yup."

"Not just at practice. Did you stay after?"

"I played at the beach courts tonight."

"Good. Did you hear about Rodriguez?"

I turn around.

"She had a thirty-thirty game last night."

I toss my duffel by my door. "Want to shoot some baskets?"

"That's my girl," he beams.

twelve

I wake up early on Sunday morning, tired from shooting hoops until all hours the night before, and push myself to run two miles on the beach. When I come home, I enter through the back door, hoping no one is there. I don't know whether it's from forcing myself to work so hard lately or from all the pressure I'm under to win that spot on the Suns and keep the Beachwood Basketball dynasty alive, but I'm beginning to feel lightheaded.

I run up the stairs and plop down on my bed, marveling at how I managed to make it successfully up to my room without a parental run-in. Just then, my dad appears at my bedroom door, wearing swim trunks, a T-shirt, and a towel around his neck. "Hey, Spider! I'm about to go out back for a swim. Want to do some drills after lunch?"

I suck in a deep breath and suppress my initial urge to turn him down. I mean, I'm absolutely beat. But, it's my dad asking, and I just don't have the heart to tell him no. "Meet you out back at one," I say.

"Perfect! That's my girl." He breaks out in a huge smile, and even though I'm beyond tired, it's worth it.

"Is mom up yet?"

"Nope. I'm sure you'll catch up with her. See you at one!" He partially closes my room door—I'm assuming so that my mom can't hear me from the master suite down the hall—and begins to make his way outside to our backyard pool.

While still lying on my bed, I toss off my Asics running sneakers, throwing them onto my light blue carpeting, wherever they happen to land. Then I calm my breathing and grab an orange foam Nerf ball from my nightstand.

"With two seconds left and down by one, Thomas has the ball in the paint." I commentate like Nancy Lieberman, holding the ball up in the air in front of me. "She fakes left. But, will she dunk?" I push myself up off the bed, spin, jump, and dunk into the basket that is hooked on the door to my walk-in closet. "Thomas did it again! And the crowd goes wild!" I jog in place and raise my arms in victory. Then I hold one arm out, pointing at the corkboard above my desk in homage to the amazing players whose pictures fill my board: Diana Taurasi, Becky Hammon, Lisa Leslie, Candace Parker, and various Olympic Dream Teams.

I throw myself down on the chocolate brown couch by my picture window, and, after a half hour of catching up on my various social networking obligations (and confirming that Zach and Kylie are both still listed as single), I decide to attack my closet. If I'm going to go through with the fashion show for Hannah, I might as well practice my strut. Assuming fashion shows are anything like basketball, the more practice, the better. Right?

Making my way to the back right of my walk-in, I find the way-too-tiny vintage *L.A. High* hand-me-downs my mom stuffed in there in case I ever wanted to "embrace my girliness."

But, can I really do this? Can I really walk the runway in front of the entire school?

Rallying myself, I pull the black-and-white Chanel strapless prom dress from *L.A. High* Season Three off the rack. Then, I channel my inner Hannah, shed my running clothes, and squeeze into the dress. Next, I pile my hair on top of my head and spritz hairspray all over to keep it in place. *I think that's how my mom does it.* The dress is super short and I can't zipper it up all the way, but I'm determined to make it work. I sashay back and forth across my closet, turn, and watch myself in my mirror. Once I'm done with my strut, I pull another dress off a hanger. Take two.

Later, my cell phone buzzes in my hand. I wipe my eyes and realize I fell asleep on my bed, dressed in my mom's designer duds. I tap my phone and wipe my eyes a second time.

FR: UNLISTED
WHATCHA DOIN? ZACH

Then, I read it over. And over. Before it registers, the phone vibrates again.

FR: UNLISTED
CAN I STOP BY?

My thumbs run over the N and O keys. He can't come over. I just woke up, and I'm sitting on my bed, with frizzy hair, in a crinkled dress. Whenever I've imagined this moment, I'm as perfectly styled as I was for the eighth grade graduation dinner when Hannah did my hair, clothes, and makeup. No way am I a hot mess. But, before I can hit send, the doorbell rings.

thirteen

I'm not the type to run around freaking out whenever I'm caught off guard with a surprise. But Zachary Murphy just dropping by? And on a day I look disgusting? That definitely calls for some major freakage.

I drop my phone and catch a glimpse of my reflection in my mirror. I stop dead in my tracks. It's worse than I imagined. I didn't realize that it was possible to attain this level of bed head. And this outfit? Forget the school fashion show. Sign me up for the circus.

My mom's voice comes through the white intercom box to the right of my closet door. "Taylor, are you in your room? There is a boy here to see you." Of course, now my mom decides to wake up.

I open my mouth to say something, but my tongue feels like it's glued to the roof of my mouth. Bad hair, nasty morning breath, and Zachary Murphy at my doorstep. Great.

For a second, I consider hiding. But, it'd be just my luck that my mom would bring Zach up here and the two of them would find me kneeling behind the shoe rack in my closet. Guess there's only one thing to do. I toss off the too-short slip dress and throw my running clothes back on. Then I pull my hair on top of my head and pop a piece of Eclipse gum into my mouth.

In super slow-mo, I turn my doorknob and open my bedroom door. I slide along the wall until I emerge in the open balcony overlooking the foyer and duck behind a giant plant. Gently, I separate two huge green leaves to take a peek.

It's him in his ultra-hotness. Zachary Murphy is in my house. As usual, he looks totally relaxed. His hands are casually tucked into his jean pockets. And his hair looks like it was ruffled just the right amount by the wind.

"Huh . . . I don't know where she is." My mom, looking kind of pasty, pushes the intercom button again. "Honey, Zachary is here to see you."

She releases the button and turns her attention back to Zach, who is busy scanning the house. I crouch even lower to avoid being spotted.

"She's probably shooting baskets with her father. They're always doing that on the weekends." She presses the outdoor intercom button. "Taylor? Taylor, you there?" Not surprisingly, there isn't any answer. You know, since I'm busy hiding behind a plant.

"Hmm . . ." she says. "Maybe she just didn't hear me. Or maybe she's upstairs after all. Let me see if I can find her." My mom's heels (guessing they're Jimmy Choo because she talks about him nonstop) tap across the ceramic-tiled floor as she makes her way to the stairs.

Uh-oh. I shrink into the wall again and begin my slide back to my room.

"Taylor Isabella Thomas, what are you doing?" My mom stands at the top of the steps with her hands on her hips. Yup, she definitely just caught the tail end of my plant maneuver.

"Shhh!" I motion for her to follow me back into my room.

"There's a smoking hot boy waiting for you at the door. Why in the world were you hiding behind a plant?" She takes a seat at my desk chair.

"Mom, please don't say 'smoking hot' ever again."

"Whatever makes my darling daughter happy. But still, you didn't answer my question." She swings her feet over to one side of the chair and looks at me conspiratorially.

I stare at her. "I don't want to see him."

"Why? Because of your hair?"

"Thanks for pointing out the obvious." I pat down the back of my hair. "No," I whisper, "because he dates one of my teammates."

"Why isn't he with her right now?" She raises one eyebrow like it's the end of a dramatic scene on *L.A. High.*

I scrunch my shoulders.

"You should at least go downstairs and talk to him. He's such a cutie! And besides, he came all the way here just to see you." She juts out her lower lip, four-year-old style.

"I can't," I whisper.

"Oh, you *are* doing this. No daughter of mine is going to turn a boy like that away without even giving him the time of day."

"*Mom* . . ."

"Taylor, sweetie, if it's that bad, then you can ask him to leave. Nicely. But at least give him a chance. For me." She juts out her lower lip even farther.

"I guess he already knows what I look like when I'm playing, and I suppose I'm wearing the same kind of stuff. . . ."

"That's my girl!" My mom smiles, pushes herself out of the chair, and leads me out of my room, into the hallway, and down the stairs.

Zach is still standing there, checking his iPhone. At least he didn't bail.

"Here she is!" My mom winks at me.

Zach looks up from his phone.

"*Heyyyyy*, Zach," I say, while awkwardly doing a little wave. (Ugh, who waves when they're standing right next to someone?)

"I'll leave you crazy kids to it, then." My mom scampers back up the stairs, and I'm pretty sure I see Zach's eyes follow her all the way into the master suite. (Have I mentioned my mother's ginormous boobs and tiny waist? Yup, guess who got her looks from her dad's side?)

I realize that the only way I'm going to salvage this visit is

Head **GAMES**

with a little one-on-one time on the court. "Want to go out back?" I ask. Before he can answer, I walk toward the sliding glass doors at the rear of our great room.

He shrugs and follows me outside.

We make our way past the patio and take the stoned path to the court. I snatch a ball off the ground and pass it to him. He sets up and shoots. *Swish.*

"Nice court, Taylor." Zach looks around as I grab the ball.

"Thanks." I pass the ball back to Zach and struggle to think of something else to say. When nothing comes to mind, I resort to, "So, what's up?" Meanwhile my brain fires question after question: *Why is he here? How does he know where I live? Does he really think I'm hot?*

"Nothing." Zach dribbles to the right side of the basket, sets up inside the three-point line, and shoots. Another swish. I retrieve the ball and pass it back to him.

In my mind, I'm jumping up and down, screaming: *Zachary Murphy is in my backyard shooting baskets! Zachary Murphy is in my backyard shooting baskets!* Over and over and over again.

On the outside, I try to remain calm. "Why'd you stop by?" I ask.

He halts mid-shot, looks at me with his giant hazel eyes, and smiles. "I just wanted to see what you're up to."

I grin back as Zach shoots again from behind the three-point line. This one banks off the backboard.

He shows off his single dimple.

I grab his rebound and set up right where he missed, square up and shoot. The ball swishes through the net.

"Nice shot. Actually, I'm here because—"

"Who's up for a pick up game?" my dad shouts, interrupting our flow as he jogs toward mid-court. "Hey, Zachary Murphy, superstar boys' center at Beachwood! How's it going?" My dad swings his arm and catches Zach's hand for a hard, manly handshake. The kind of handshake I've only seen him do with his golfing buddies.

"Hi, Mr. Thomas."

"Call me Mike."

No. Oh please, no.

"Uhhh . . . nice to meet you, Mike."

Noooooo. My Zachary Murphy dream is turning into a Zachary Murphy nightmare.

Head GAMES

"This is perfect! Exactly what Taylor needs. The best boys' center at Beachwood versus the best girls' center." My dad snatches the ball from my hands. "Okay, kiddo, you set up underneath the basket." He tucks the ball underneath his arm and points with his other hand. "Zach you're on D to start. Let's see what you've got."

No. Not Zach and me one-on-one in front of my dad. *Could this get any worse?* That means Zach and I are going to be super close, touching in front of my dad. Which is (a) gross (because my dad's there) and (b) totally distracting. *But*, I really want to show Zach my skills once and for all. At least then after he confesses his deep love for all things Hannah, I already kicked his butt on the court.

I maneuver underneath the basket and my dad bounce-passes me the ball. Zach sets up behind me, and I can feel the heat from his breath on the nape of my neck. He leans in and chills run down my spine. But the mood is quickly cut short by my dad yelling, "Use your hips, Spider. Fake him out."

I move toward the right. Then I jut to the left, jump, and hit the ball softly off the backboard. *Swish.*

"Nice move, Spider!" Zach says, winking at me. The sunlight reflects off his sparkling eye-sprinkles as he retrieves the ball.

"Make it, take it." My dad snatches the ball back, completely shocking Zach.

Ohmigod. He did not just do that.

Zach and I get into position, and my dad chest passes the ball back to me. I turn around and am now face-to-face with Zach. I fake left. Drive right. And get blocked by Zach after only two dribbles. Then I set up for a jump shot, fake, and shoot. Again, no good. Zach blocks it, midair. After retrieving the deflection, he dribbles to the foul line.

"Taylor, what were you thinking?" my dad screams.

I gulp. During big games, I rise to the occasion. But, for some reason, I'm tanking in my own backyard. There's only one explanation: Zachary Murphy.

"Taylor, you just did that move! You have to use everything you have, not rely on the same footwork. How do you expect to beat Rodriguez?" my dad rants.

Mortified, I look over at Zach, afraid to see his reaction to my dad's lecture. I can't believe I pushed myself to hang out with him despite my hideous appearance, and this is how our afternoon ends.

But, it turns out that Zach isn't paying attention. He's busy texting.

Zach looks up from the screen, having realized that the court has gone silent. The only remaining sound comes from his phone. For a moment, our eyes meet and I think we might just be able to get back to our game. Maybe we'll even play a little more one-on-one. But then, my dreams are shattered by three simple words: "I gotta go."

My stomach drops. Of course, Zach has popular people to hang out with. Who am I kidding?

Zach walks up to my dad. "Nice to meet you, Mr., uhhh, Mike." He shakes my father's hand and shoves his phone back in his pocket, as my dad returns to shooting hoops. Then Zach begins to make the trek back up the path toward the house. All of a sudden, he stops, as if reconsidering. He turns back around, looking at me. "Wanna come?"

WHAT??? Did Zachary Michael Murphy just ask me to go somewhere with him? *After* hearing my dad reprimand me? *And* seeing me look like I'd been run over by a truck? *WHAT???*

I catch my breath. "Uh. Yeah." I force myself to make eye contact with him.

"Cool," he replies.

We walk through the sliding glass doors into the house and make our way to the front door. As we're about to leave, I turn to him, "Actually, would you mind waiting down here for one sec while I run upstairs?"

There's no way I'm leaving the house without first brushing my teeth. Because if he kissed my knee, maybe my lips will be next.

fifteen

"I had fun, Spider," Zach grins mischievously. He stays a few steps ahead of me, and I find my eyes drifting down to his perfectly shaped butt and the way that his legs seem to glide ever so effortlessly over the beach path. Guys like Zach even walk flawlessly.

"Sorry about my dad."

"Nah, your dad's pretty cool."

Zach might walk amazingly, but he's definitely losing it. "Seriously?" I lock eyes with Zach. *Who would chose to hang out with my dad? Let alone call him cool.*

"Yeah," he says, showing off his adorable dimple. "He's really into basketball."

"Yeah, I guess," I answer, shifting my eyes away toward the pinks and yellows being spilled by the setting sun.

We're silent for a few seconds when Zach yells out, "Hey, watch this!" Then he jumps over the boardwalk railing, landing feet first on the sand.

I take one look at the stairs and decide that I didn't attend all those training sessions for nothing. Mimicking Zach, I bound over the railing. "And she sticks it!" I call out.

Zach looks up from shedding his Jordans. "Oh, I missed it. Cool."

My brief moment of bravado comes to a crashing halt. Suddenly, I remember that this is Zach I'm with, and little feats like jumping over a railing mean nothing to him. I hesitantly slide my sneaks off and sink my toes into the cool sand.

Again, I silently count, *one Mississippi, two Mississippi . . .* The lull in the conversation begins to bother me, and I scan my brain for something amazing to say. But, all I can seem to come up with is *Kylie, Kylie, Kylie.* More basketball it is.

I turn to Zach. "Friday's Richland. If we win, we snag first place in the division for the fifth year in a row and we make the playoffs. Plus, the SoCal Suns club coaches will be in the stands."

"Yeah." He stares off into the distance. "This year's huge."

"Yup . . ." I smile, proud of my basketball skills.

"Definitely need to be prepared for Chris Garrison. He's the best guy in the league. Heard he's dunking two or three times a game."

Who the heck is Chris Garrison? My toes sink deeper into the sand as we walk along the shoreline. Steeling my nerves, I hear the wind howling in the background. *Oh, that explains it.* He probably didn't hear me over the breeze.

"But, Coach says I'll get major exposure if I score big this game. I heard *SI* might even be there since Garrison is the number two high school recruit in the country." He breaks out in a huge grin. Even bigger than the one usually plastered across his face when he's hanging off the rim. "Can you imagine? Me in *SI*? That's Lebron status."

If we're talking Lebron status, I guess I can overlook his mishearing me.

He grabs my hand and pulls me toward the surf. "Want to swim?"

"Uhhh, uhhh . . ." I look down at my white tee. "I don't think that's such a good idea. I don't have a bathing suit. And, you know, it's February—"

"Dude, it's warm out. The water's fine. And who cares about bathing suits?" Zach lifts his black Beachwood tee up over his head, revealing his extremely tan, extremely muscular chest. YUMMY. Next, he pulls his jeans down to expose his (yikes) white mesh shorts. Finally, he tosses his phone and Movado watch on top of his sneaks and dives into a wave. When he emerges, he shakes out his hair. Beads of water spray off. My mouth drops open.

"You coming in?" He grins. "It's nice out here." Then he plunges back underwater.

He *did* ask me. And I wouldn't want to hurt his feelings. . . . Plus, I'm pretty sure no girl would ever refuse a dip in the ocean with someone who has abs like Zach's. *But*, there's still the Kylie issue.

"Come on." He smiles. My heart's beating so fast, I swear it's going to explode. This is my big moment. Who knows when I'll have another opportunity like this? *Kylie, please forgive me.* I leave my clothes on and jump in.

Zach pops his head up out of the water, smiling roguishly. "That's my girl."

His girl? *Melt.*

We splash and giggle for a bit. Then he wraps his bulky arms around my shoulders and looks deep into my eyes as we bob up and down with the water. "Do you think we're good together?"

I nod.

"Yeah, me too. You're the only girl at Beachwood who can really school the competition out on the court. You're like the girl-me."

Totally and completely melting, I nod again.

He begins to lean toward me. This is it. The event I've been waiting for. The one that will take me from inexperienced, awkward Towering Taylor Thomas to Taylor Thomas: basketball superstar by day, girl-who's-been-kissed by night. I shut my eyes.

And—bang! Instead of Zach's full lips, a huge wave slams into me. Salt water shoots up my nose and I'm pulled underwater. I try to tread, but I'm gagging and coughing so much, I can't make it to the surface. I wave my arms above the water, mentally pleading, *Zach, help!*

Finally, I feel him grab my hand and pull me to the shoreline.

Gasping for breath, I push against the sand and attempt to

sit up. My knee screams. Between the salt and the sand, my cut's a mess. That's when I notice that Zach is doubled over laughing.

I look at him.

"You okay?" he asks, between fits of giggles.

This is *so* not funny. I could have died. The one time I do something for myself, and sure enough, a wave decides to topple me over. Serves me right for *ever* being so selfish. *How on Earth am I going to make it up to Kylie?*

sixteen

It's happened. Zach's face has officially turned pink from laughing so hard.

Meanwhile, I've given up on my attempts to sit up straight and have resumed my original lying-flat-on-the-wet-sand position. My coughs are now coming in spurts, but my throat and nose still burn intensely.

"Come on. Time to sit up for real." In one full swoop, Zach pushes my shoulders up off the ground (causing me to awkwardly fall forward) and grabs his tee and Movado. He checks the time and nods to himself. Turning back to me, he asks, "How about some more one-on-one?"

I shrug my shoulders, and, using all my energy, manage to stand up. Then, I follow Zach toward the beach court. As he's retrieving a ball that's been deserted near the bleachers, I pull my drenched hair back into a ponytail and make a silent vow: *No more Miss Nice Girl. I will show Zachary Murphy what I'm made of.*

"Make it, take it." He bounce-passes me the ball and again shows off those blindingly white teeth. "Maybe today you can stay on your feet."

"Whatever." I dribble, switching hands, and keep his gaze. Then, I pull up and take a three.

Swish.

See, this is okay. I just took a little swim with Zach. Now we're playing some basketball. No big deal. Kylie won't be upset. The team's still intact. We're just friends. Friends hanging out shooting baskets. Completely innocent. Well, except for the fact that I'm going to kick some major Murphy butt.

"Nice shot," Zach says, retrieving the ball. He bounce-passes it back to me and I immediately drive past him, laying the ball into the net left-handed. Turning around, I expect some serious applause. I mean, that's the move I'm going to use to beat Rodriguez on Friday. It's pretty unbelievable (if I do say so myself). But, something on Zach's phone seems to have caught his attention.

"I gotta go," he says, shoving the phone back into his back pocket.

Right, his plans. "I guess I won," I announce, somewhat timidly. My original suspicion was correct. Of course Zach would have more exciting things to do than hang out with me. While retrieving the ball, I take a deep breath and force myself to see the good in the situation. With Zach leaving, I can go on with my life without worrying about Kylie. No hook-up. No problem.

Still, part of me wants to say something to him about the whole making-it-seem-like-he-was-inviting-me-to-go-out-with-his-friends-but-not-really thing. But, as I turn around, I see that Zach is standing directly in front of me.

He looks straight at me, and, before I realize what the heck is happening, he pulls me in and presses his warm lips against mine. *Finally.* My whole body tingles. He grabs my waist and lures me closer, diving deeper into my mouth.

We pull apart and I'm breathless. *Wait? Did that just happen? Oh. My. God. Scratch that. Oh my Zachary Michael Murphy.*

Grabbing the rest of his belongings, he says, "I'll text you later." And with that, he jogs toward the dunes and disappears.

What does this mean??? Besides, you know, that my cause of death has now become clear to me: murdered by Kylie Collins. I stare at the backboard. Then, I scan the court, having been suddenly overwhelmed by a serious urge to shoot baskets. That's when my next realization hits: Zach just took the ball.

seventeen

"It's all over Beachwood!" Hannah announces, the next day after first period.

"See you tomorrow, Pat," I say, leaving a copy of my history notes on his desk. Patrick is ranked third in our class and doesn't really need the help. But because of his wheelchair, he has to leave every class early so that he can make it through the hallways without being stopped by the crazy in-between-class traffic. And sometimes he misses little things, like a few history notes.

"Thanks, Tay," he says, grinning at me and pulling the desk toward him.

I turn my attention toward Hannah as we begin walking toward my locker. "What's all over Beachwood?" I ask, feeling my brand new, ruby-red patent leather heels slip off my feet. They look super cute with Vi's skinny jeans (just like she said they would) and my basketball warm-up jacket. (Okay, so Vi told me to pair the outfit with a blazer, but I don't exactly own one of those and Hannah's doesn't fit).

"You and—" She pauses and looks down at my shoes as I balance myself against my locker. "What the heck are on your feet, Dorothy?"

"My heels!" I exclaim, catching myself mid-teeter.

"Oh." She gives me her "you're strange" look. As I'm about to remind her that she's the one who's pushing me to be Beachwood's next fashionista, her expression shifts. "Wait. Don't tell me you're practicing for the show?"

"Uh, yeah. Who's the greatest best friend ever?"

"Well, that's a hard call. When you look at a friendship like Kylie and Missy's, I just don't know if ours can compare."

"Haha. Very funny. So, anyway, the suspense is killing me. What's all over school???" My hand-me-down Louis Vuitton bag (the one I found yesterday in my mom's closet while she was out "working" AGAIN) slides off my shoulder. This fashion thing might just be even harder than it looks.

Hannah's blue eyes bug out. "Only that a certain Zachary Michael Murphy was at your house yesterday."

"And?"

"And that after shooting some hoops, you guys took a little stroll on the beach."

"A stroll?"

"You're right. A stroll doesn't really cover it. Let's back it up. You and Zach went to the beach and did some serious tongue wrestling."

"Ohmigod."

"Yeah, oh my god is right. How could you not tell me??? *Me?* Your best friend. The girl who you played Bratz dolls with when you were little."

"No, oh my god—Kylie."

"Oh, that's the best part. I heard he's totally done with Kylie."

"Wait. What?!? Who told you that?" I scream. *Wayyy* too loud. Instinctively, I cover my mouth with one hand and begin fumbling with my locker with the other.

"The *entire* school knows. Well, that and the fact that you're Zach's latest hook-up. *Are you?*" Hannah almost does a little jump, but stops herself when she notices Vi sauntering down the hallway. She's sporting a new look today too—chocolate brown hair for the fashion show. Hannah turns back to me. "Anyway, spill, girl, spill."

"Yeah, sure. In a sec. But, first, tell me: Has Kylie heard about us?" I ask. As the words leave my lips, I'm not sure if I really want to know the answer.

"Uhhh . . ."

Great. Even Hannah's nervous. Bracing myself for the big reveal, I decide to play it cool. I turn around and calmly open my locker. That's when I see it. *SKANK*. The word is scratched across the inside, marring the blue paint.

"I guess that answers your question," Hannah says, grabbing my Asics out of my locker and thrusting them at me. "You're gonna need these if you plan on outrunning Kylie."

I take a deep breath and slowly step out of my heels, one foot at a time. As I bend down to put on my sneakers, Vi's jeans slice into my stomach. After casting a quick glance

Head GAMES

around to double check that no one other than Hannah is looking, I bend down and play with the waistband, causing my handbag to slip off my arm and land on the floor. This is not good. Not good at all. And this is *exactly* what happens when I'm not nice.

eighteen

"Good morning, class, please take out your Word-of-the-Day assignments," Mr. Ludwig, our English teacher, announces.

While Mr. Ludwig drones on and on about the importance of this project "in light of the widespread cultural failure to impress upon our nation's youth the vital significance of acquiring an extensive and sophisticated vocabulary," I unhook the top button of my jeans. Then I begin staring at Mr. Ludwig's shiny bald spot, and ask myself the same question I pose every day: In what cruel world would I not end up with Martie for English?

Today, however, my thoughts swerve, eventually landing on one person in particular: Zach. Why was it that he came over my house? Why did he kiss me? Does he really like me? Why did he change his status back to "in a relationship" as of ten fifty-eight last night? Did something happen? And who is he in a relationship with? *Is it me?*

Just to be sure, I pull out my phone, hide it beneath my desk, and change my status to "in a relationship." But, then I change it back to single again. And then I switch it sixteen more times before I finally settle on single.

Ughhh. *I just don't know anymore.* I open my notebook and begin writing in the hopes that a list might clear things up.

Reasons Zachary Murphy Came Over and Kissed Me:

1. He saw the basketball court and wanted to play.
2. He needs someone six feet or over to practice basketball with.
3. He was curious to see if my parents were huge and gigantic like me (and if we are part of the circus or something).
4. He wants to see how much psychotic behavior Kylie is capable of.
5. He's a closet fan of *L.A. High* who watches reruns on the SOAP network and wanted to meet my mom.
6. He's in a relationship with me!!!! (*although highly unlikely) ☺

"Okay, share with your partner," Mr. Ludwig calls out.

Matt taps me on my shoulder. "Hey, Taylor, what's your word?"

I spin around and face Matt, hiding my list as I flip to my homework. When I look up from my notebook, his brown eyes meet mine. A gray Beachwood Academy Lacrosse hoodie (can't stress how much he loves his hoodies) hugs his thick, tan neck and a sweet smile graces his lips. If only he were about four inches taller! But, alas, he only meets two of my three boyfriend requirements. And height is numero uno.

Plus, he's with Violet. And they look perfect together. Of course. And let's not forget his illicit past . . .

"You first," I say.

"No, you. I want to hear this." Matt grins and leans back in his chair. "Let me guess, it's about Murph." He crosses his arms in front of his chest.

"Whatever." I smile and attempt a peek at Matt's open notebook. Naturally, he catches me in the act.

"Umm Taylor, this is some serious stuff. If I allow you to discover my Word of the Day before I'm ready, I might just be damaged for life. And if I were that traumatized, I might need to switch classes. And if I did that, who would you talk to during English?"

"Someone who actually did his homework."

"Ouch. Now you've asked for it. Prepare to be awed and amazed."

"Lucky me. I finally get to learn your secret."

Matt glances at me oddly, and I realize that I've committed a serious sin. Matt, after all, does have *real* secrets. "Uhh, so what's your word?" I ask, attempting to redirect.

"*Polemic*, noun," he plays with the page in his notebook.

"And why did you pick *polemic*?" I regurgitate the question from the worksheet script Mr. Ludwig gave us last month.

"It means to engage in a controversial argument. And—"

I cut him off. "Let me guess. Gray hoodies are super controversial."

"You'd be surprised. Actually, on Saturday, my lacrosse coach engaged in a very controversial argument over a call. See, the ref called us offsides and we weren't. We ended up down a man because one of the guys on the team argued it."

"Uh-oh. I think I know where this is going," I interject.

"Yeah. As I'm sure you've guessed, the other team scored because we were shorthanded."

"And how many points did you lose by?" I ask, even after I do the math in my head.

"One. Of course." Matt shrugs.

"Sheesh. That blows," I commiserate.

"Yup, it does," Matt agrees, looking at me. For a second, I think that maybe venting made Matt feel better. But the calm doesn't last. "What's your word? *Murph?*" Matt asks, mocking me.

"Nooooo. It's . . . uh . . ." I spot the corner of what appears to be a diary underneath Matt's English notebook. I thought only girls wrote in diaries. Not burly, thick Matt-types. "Is that a journal?" I ask, pulling at the black leather edge.

Matt's eyes widen and he leans against the pile on his desk. "It's nothing."

"Oooh, come on. Let me see." I snag it, causing his books to tumble.

Opening the book, I notice right away that tons of short poems grace the pages. *What???*

Chocolate

My girl is milk chocolate.

Always sweet, never bitter.

Just like the sound of her voice, her life, her looks.

Always sweet, never bitter.

I flip to another page.

Why?

He's so wrong for her.

In so many ways.

Why can't she be with me?

Instead, she stays.

And another.

Dad

What does it mean to be a dad?

To push and pull.

      Pull and push.

Until I can't breathe.

Until I break.

Until I bleed.

And quit the only thing I'm good at.

Wow. I look up at Matt and then back down at the pages. I'm at a total loss for what to say. His poems are all amazing. I can't believe that one about his dad. I had no idea he was so tough on him. And *whoa*, that "Chocolate" poem. If only someone would write poetry like that about me. . . . Vi is so lucky. Who knew her new hair-do would lead to this?

Sensing my silence, Matt attempts to grab the notebook, but I play defense, turning my back to block him out.

Matt kind of harrumphs at me.

Not one to relish upsetting people, I'm tempted to return the journal then and there. But I just can't bring myself to do it. I decide to be direct. "Matt, these are really good," I say. "I never knew you were a poet."

"Yeah. I—"

"And that 'Chocolate' poem? Vi must love it."

Matt turns ruby red, reaches around my back, and snatches the journal. "Look, Taylor, don't tell anyone that you read these, okay? The guys on the team would have a field day if they knew."

"I guess so, tough guy." I giggle, pinching his bicep.

Matt squirms.

"How long have you been writing poetry?" I ask, wondering how he kept it under wraps for so long. I mean, the guys on the lacrosse team hang out together constantly.

"I don't know. A while, I guess." He looks around the classroom, shoves the journal back underneath his books, and wipes his forehead.

"It's crazy hot in here." He wipes his face again, pushes his sleeves up to his elbows, and clenches his fists.

"Nah. It's just you," I say and giggle, hoping to make him feel comfortable again. I hate to see anyone squirm.

"Feisty, are we?" he replies.

"Only when you're around." I wink.

"So . . ." He relaxes back in his seat. "Who are you playing today?"

"Bel Air," I answer. "They kind of stink, but Friday's game against Richland is *huge*." My stomach flips just thinking about Friday.

"What's going on Friday?" Matt leans forward.

"The coach of an elite regional summer club team, the SoCal Suns, is going to be there," I explain. "And if we win against Richland, our three-peat should be a piece of cake."

"That's awesome."

"Yeah, the SoCals are AH-mazing. Last year, three girls from the team went on to work out with the Olympic Development Program." I wave my hands, animatedly.

"Really?" Matt asks.

"Yup, and all of the players end up going to big-time colleges." I literally bounce in my seat.

"Excited much?" Matt teases me.

"Oh yeah. But it's not like a spot with them is in the bag or anything."

"What are you talking about? I'm sure that the great Taylor Thomas will blow away any scout."

"Well, the problem is the team we're playing on Friday. Or, more specifically, their center: Rodriguez."

"I'm sure this Rodriguez can't match your mad skillz."

"Oh, is that right, home skillet?"

"You know it."

"Honestly, Rodriguez is definitely a contender for the spot."

"Okay, so you'll show her who's boss when the time comes."

"I hope so. But that's not the only reason why this game is *sooo* huge. If we beat Richland, we pretty much clinch the division. If we lose ..." I cross my fingers. "Then, the Beachwood dynasty comes crashing down."

"Wow. A lot riding on one game." Matt smiles. "Good luck."

"I'll need it."

"Sounds like that's up for debate." Matt's smile grows wider.

I grin back.

Continuing, Matt takes one final jab, "So, tell me Taylor Thomas, with all this basketball stuff going on, how do you have time for your boy Murph?"

Now, I'm the one who's ruby.

nineteen

"Skank!" Kylie yells from across the cafeteria.

"Neeeiiiigggghhhh," Missy and Brooke call out in between strawberry lip-gloss applications. Gotta love the horse nickname. Nick christened me with that one during the second grade. With my long, lanky legs and mane of chestnut brown hair, he insisted I was born a calf.

The at-ease feeling I had from hanging out with Matt doesn't last long. Right now, at lunchtime, Kylie and her crew are involved in Operation Humiliate Taylor Thomas. Who knew the kiss rumor would spread even faster than the ultra-embarrassing Chloe Simpson cell phone pic Kylie sent to everyone last year? I throw down my second water bottle in less than ten minutes, attempting to make my mouth taste less like sandpaper.

"Don't listen to them," Hannah yells over the neighs, snorts, and giggles. "They're just jealous." She rolls her eyes and shovels a spoon of organic peanut butter into her mouth. Then she looks up just in time to see me mouth, "I'm sorry" to Kylie's table.

Not one to let me get away with my "pay-it-forward"

method, she immediately calls me out. "You did not just tell Kylie and her band of bumbling bimbos that you're sorry, did you?"

"Uh, well, you know, I can't help it!" I respond.

"Tay. Come on. Give it up already. You can be sweet all you want. It's not like Kylie and Co. are going to care."

"Maybe they'll have a change of heart. Kylie used to be nice."

"That was before. Anyway, enough Kylie talk. Are you going to give me the deets on the kiss or what?"

"It was no big deal," I insist.

"No big deal? Was it good?" Hannah asks, refusing to believe that I told her the whole story.

I shrug. "Sort of."

"What do you mean 'sort of'?" Hannah has now begun licking the spoon.

"Nothing," I say, staring at my turkey-and-cheese-with-honey-mustard wrap. Unlike Hannah, I buy my lunch at the cafeteria.

"Nothing?" Hannah gives me an I'm-not-buying-your-story look.

"I mean, it was okay."

"Okay. What do you mean 'okay'?" Hannah's eyes enlarge. "This is Zachary Murphy. *The* Zachary Murphy."

I put my hands on the table and lean over to her. "Yes, it was amazing and sparkly and everything I thought it would be."

Looking satisfied, Hannah takes a violent bite out of a piece of bread she clearly swiped from Panera. (She maintains that the sample baskets are there for your eating pleasure. I maintain that they're there actually for *sampling*.) Brushing off the crumbs that land on her lap, she catches notice of her Volcom bag. Her eyes widen. "Ooh, I almost forgot." She opens the bag and pulls out a piece of tan shearling. "What do you think of this?"

I don't answer. I'm too busy watching Zach feed a dollar into the Aquafina machine and thinking to myself: *I kissed him! I kissed him!*

"Tay, are you even listening?"

I continue to stare.

"Earth to Taylor!"

I notice that Kylie has joined Zach at the Aquafina machine and avert my eyes. "Uh, what is it?"

"Way to pay attention," Hannah chides me.

"Sorry, I—uh—got distracted."

"No kidding. But, to answer your question, I got it off one of Vi's old Ugg handbags," she says, smugly.

"One of these days, Vi is gonna kill ya." I wag my finger at her in mock disapproval.

"I know." She smirks. Then she hands the fabric over to me.

"Wow. It's really soft. What are you doing with this?"

Hannah snorts her Red Bull. "I'm gonna shove it up my butt hole. What do you mean what am I doing with it? It's for my design."

"Oh, yeah. That's . . ." My thoughts are interrupted by the sounds of Kylie and Zach laughing. "Look," I say, nodding in their direction.

Hannah turns around. "What?"

"I'll bet they're back together by tomorrow."

"Oh, Tay." Hannah sighs. "Maybe you're wrong and it's not what it looks like."

On cue, Kylie's arms flail around. Zach, looking ever so slightly irritated, takes a relaxed swig from his water bottle and walks away, leaving Kylie standing alone by the machine.

Hannah turns back around. "I'll never understand the two of them. They're clearly oil and water." She takes another bite out of her bread. "Now, you on the other hand, I'm extremely proud of."

"Seriously?" I look at Hannah, disbelievingly.

"Yeah. I mean, you're the girl who's nice to everyone she meets. Who comments on *every* single post. And to totally disregard Kylie and go after Zach? That takes some serious cojones."

"Are you saying that I don't normally have cojones?"

"You do on the court, but—"

"But, I know, you don't have to say it. I . . ." I lose my train of thought when I spot a school store sign advertising Matt's fave sweatshirt. Turning back to Hannah, I decide that I need to know the truth once and for all. "Banana, I have to ask you something, and I want you to answer me honestly. Is Matt hooking up with Vi?"

"Matt Moore?" Hannah grins. "Matt's so sweet. And—"

But before she can finish her answer, Zach plops down in the vacant seat next to her.

"*Heyyyy*," Hannah says, all nonchalant.

Zach gives Hannah a little nod and then turns to me. "Hey, Taylor. What's up?"

Hannah juts her head forward. She doesn't like being ignored. "My designs."

As they're talking, I start trembling, just thinking about what Kylie will do to me when she finds out that Zach made his way over to my table after abandoning her at the Aquafina machine.

Hannah gestures in my direction. "And my complicated model."

Zach looks at me and smiles. "I think your model is perfect."

At this point, I'm shuddering so wildly, I'm wondering why no one's called the nurse.

"Uh, thanks," I say, rallying myself. Then I go quiet.

Attempting to resuscitate the convo, Hannah asks, "Want to hear what my line's called?"

Zach tosses his Aquafina bottle in the air. Catching it, he asks, "What's it called?"

"Banana Fad." Hannah smiles at me.

"Like the fruit?" Zach squeezes his water bottle.

"It's a Taylor-me thing," Hannah replies, pointing at me and then at herself as if we're in a gang of two.

And then my worst fears are realized. Kylie has spotted us.

Standing at the head of the cafeteria table, she bangs and shouts, "How can you guys do this to me?" The table shakes. Plates, bottles, and other random items rattle. But Kylie doesn't seem to care. Thrusting her head at Zach, she squeals, "She's my teammate!"

With those words, I begin to lose track of what Kylie and Zach are saying. The cafeteria spins, and, for a sec, all I hear is a steady buzzing of voices. *How could I have been so selfish? She's right. We are teammates. Oh my god. Oh my god. Oh my god.*

"Kylie, calm down," Zach says.

"No, I'm not going to calm down. You guys make me sick." She stamps her foot, forcefully.

When will this be over? I need to find a way to fix things. I gather my strength and look at Kylie. "Listen, Kylie, I'm really sorry that I hurt you. I'll seriously do anything to make this up to you."

In super slow-mo, Kylie turns to face me. "*What???*"

"It's just that I—" Looking up at Kylie, I catch a pained expression cross her face. But then, it's gone, just as quickly as it came. Replaced by her classic venomous stare. "I—"

"Taylor, you made out with the guy who was supposed to be my boyfriend. Or at least I thought he was. What could you ever possibly do to make up for betraying me like that?"

"I—"

Zach and Hannah look back and forth between me and Kylie, their eyes like saucers.

Brrrring. Brrrring. Brrrring. Saved by the bell.

twenty

Usually my fave days are game days, but today I'm dragging because of the constant whispers and eye daggers from Kylie and her crew. Since the nice approach isn't working real well, I avoid her as much as possible during the school day. But, come game time, I have no choice but to meet her face-to-face.

So, after school I calmly approach her to try to talk everything out one-on-one, thinking that maybe we can continue the conversation we started earlier in the caf. *However*, whatever moment we had before is gone completely. She's not having my apology. If anything, it seems like my efforts only make things worse. You know, because she ends up yelling "skank" (again) and turning her back to me. Turns out that tracking someone down to talk things out is not always such a great idea.

The game starts off just as bad as I'd imagined. After only scoring two points in the first half, we're losing to Bel Air, who totally suck, by six. It's not my playing ability that is lacking. Nope, Kylie is barely passing me the ball. Seriously. And it's a basic rule of basketball: Without the guard passing the center the ball, the team is screwed.

Unfortunately, none of this seems to matter to Kylie. Who cares if I'm open? All day long. Or that with Bel Air's tallest player being Hannah's size, there's no chance of anyone blocking me? Eventually, even our fans begin to notice that something's up. Four minutes in, they start shouting, "Taylor's open!" and "Pass the ball to Taylor!"

Halftime comes around, and the team trails into the locker room, our heads hung low. We know that we're in for it. Sure enough, Coach Jackson stamps inside, lets out a deep breath, and begins furiously scribbling on the large whiteboard. Coach Martie follows close behind, sits down, and runs her hands through her short, black hair. Throwing the blue marker down on the whiteboard ledge, Coach Jackson turns and slams the door shut.

"What the heck is going on?" she screams, looking at Kylie and then at me. She tosses her blue suit jacket on a chair. "Kylie, you and Taylor are supposed to be executing plays together, and she's obviously open, but you're not passing her the ball!"

Kylie stares blankly at Coach. I slide down in my seat.

"Why would you blow the game on purpose?" Coach glares at Kylie.

Kylie shrugs her shoulders.

Bam.

Coach smashes her plastic clipboard against her desk and pushes up her white dress sleeves. "And Taylor, whatever is going on between you and Kylie, you two better make it right before you get back out there on the court. If you don't, be sure to bring your running sneakers to practice tomorrow because we won't stop running until this mess is over. We have no time for this ridiculousness." Coach storms out of the room, slamming the door behind her.

Martie lingers for a bit. "Think about this for a second. No one person wins a championship. A team does." Then, she slinks out.

A flush of heat torpedoes through my body. I messed up. Big time.

Finally, Tamika, our senior captain, speaks up. "Coach has a point, guys." She looks at both of us. "We all know what happened with Zach this weekend, but Kylie, you need to put that aside for the team. Without Taylor scoring, we're not going to win. And if Taylor doesn't get the ball, she's not going to score." Tamika glares at me. "Not that I agree with what you did, Taylor; it was totally messed up."

My face burns with shame.

Tamika turns to Kylie, tucking a skinny braid into her ponytail. "Can't you put this Zach mess aside for the team?"

"For the team, yeah." She looks at Tamika, then at me.

Tamika shifts her glare to me. "And Taylor, what do you have to say to Kylie?"

"Sorry, Kylie. I really do want to make this right," I say, even though I've already tried this strategy. But at this point I just don't know what else to tell her.

"Okay, Kylie. She said she's sorry." Tamika places her

hands on her hips. "Now, let's put this behind us and win this game."

Kylie glowers at her.

"Come on," Tamika pleads, "we worked too hard this season to blow it today against a team as bad as Bel Air."

"Whatever." Kylie rolls her eyes.

The buzzer sounds and we file out of the locker room toward the court.

"She'll get over it," Jessica whispers, as she jogs by.

But, I don't believe Jessica. I screwed up royally. Good-bye, three-peat. Good-bye, SoCals. Good bye, friends. Good-bye, Zach. Hello, self-induced purgatory.

twenty-one

Even though we played super sloppy during the first half, when we get back out on the court, I immediately sense that this quarter is going to be different. Sure enough, Kylie begins reluctantly passing me the ball, and I easily nail nine baskets and three free throws in fifteen minutes. *Maybe I can make this right.*

"Three," Kylie shouts, dribbling the ball across half-court and holding up three fingers.

Tamika looks at me. Then she nods, signaling the play. I run her way and she picks off my defender. Kylie passes me the ball. The defender maneuvers around Tamika, emerging in front of me. Using every square inch of my height, I square up and shoot over the defender's outstretched arms. *Swish.*

And then, I turn around and spot him. Sitting and chatting with my dad is Zach. I stop and stare, shaking my head. At first, I think maybe I'm hallucinating, but when a Bel Air jersey runs by and scores, I notice that Kylie has also stopped dead in her tracks.

Coach Jackson goes nuts. "Get back in the game, you two!" she shouts from the bench. "Get your heads in the game!"

I turn around and jog back to my position

"Five," Kylie shouts with pursed lips, glaring at me while she holds up her fingers.

Tamika cuts to the foul line. Kylie passes her the ball. I post for position underneath the basket with my hands up. Tamika passes me the ball, I drop step and turn toward the basket, but the basket's moving and my steps are all wrong. When I go in for my layup, the ball bounces off the backboard and ricochets right into Bel Air's hands.

All of a sudden, I can't breathe. I can barely see. My heart is pounding. My mouth is dry. *Am I losing it because of all this Kylie drama? I mean, it isn't like this is my first game. What is wrong with me?*

I sprint back to a defensive position. Bel Air takes a jump shot from inside the paint. I jump up and grab the blurry orange blur. Then, I stop for a second to shake my head. And during that short second, Bel Air steals the ball and shoots. *Swish.*

In the distance, I can hear my dad and Coach screaming at me. But the gym is fuzzy and everything is back to slow-mo. *Stop feeling like this. It's just Kylie. It's just a little drama. It will pass.*

The buzzer sounds and Abby, another Beachwood freshman player, jogs my way and slaps my hand, taking my spot on the court. I stagger to the sideline and sit on a cold metal folding chair as far away from Coach Jackson as possible.

"Taylor, get over here." Coach points to the chair next to her.

With my head down, I slowly amble over.

Coach shouts directions to the team and then leans toward me. "What is going on with you out there?"

"I don't know," I say, staring at my black Nikes Vis Air Elites.

"You're completely out of it."

"I know."

"Do you want to start? Do you want to play basketball in college?"

I nod. The fuzziness begins to lift.

"What?" She cups her ear and tilts towards me.

"Yes, I do," I answer.

"Are you sick?"

"I don't think so, Coach." I think back to how the gym went all funny.

"Then, get yourself together. My job is to put the best girls out on the court. I need someone out there who wants to play and is going to give it one hundred percent. Not fight with teammates, gaze at the stands, give the ball away, and blow layups. I'll bench you for the rest of the season and you can kiss basketball good-bye. Do you understand me? There are plenty of other girls waiting to take your spot. Abby, for instance." She nods at Abby's whirling form.

"Okay," I squeak. A few tears drip down my face. I've heard Coach lay into players before, but never me and never this bad.

Coach shakes her head, and then, catching sight of Kylie fouling a Bel Air player, jumps out of her seat and returns to screaming directions at the team.

Martie maneuvers over and places a hand on my shoulder. "Whatever is going on, I'm here if you need to talk."

I squeak a quick, "Thanks," more mortified than ever. Then, I get up, move as far away from my coaches as possible, and grab a towel. After I wipe my face, drying the tears from my cheeks, I try to focus my eyes. That's when I look up at the bleachers and spot my dad, shaking his head.

A realization dawns on me. I'm not only the source of all this drama. I'm the worst daughter *ever.*

twenty-two

After the game ends, and we run ten suicides (even though we eventually won by three, Coach was *not* happy), I hightail it out of the locker room, wondering why I'm feeling crazy stressed. Before I can make it too far, Tamika startles me by shouting, "Everyone, in the team room. Now."

It's never a good idea to irritate Tamika, so I shuffle into the team room along with the rest of my teammates. Guess I can spend time mulling over my bad game later.

Tamika takes Coach's spot in front of the whiteboard. "Okay. This has got to stop," she says, crossing her arms.

Uh-oh. I know where this conversation is going.

"Lately we stink." Tamika's looks around the room, allowing the intensity of her words to sink in. "And it's all because of guys."

I put my head down and stare at my hands.

"Do you think the guys' team is blowing games because of us? Not likely." Tamika stares at Kylie, then Missy, and then me.

"Missy, you've been playing terrible lately."

Missy looks up from her compact mirror and twists her lip-gloss tube closed. She clicks her mirror shut.

"And can you honestly tell me it isn't because of Andrew Mason?"

Andrew Mason is a senior guard on the basketball team (too short for me by three inches but still cute) who Missy has been eyeing since last month's beach bonfire.

She looks down at her hands. "Yeah, I guess I've been distracted."

"Exactly." Tamika looks at Kylie. "And Kylie. What about Saturday's drama with Jessica?" She nods at Jessica. "And it was a total rumor. Not even true. All that fuss for nothing."

Kylie rolls her eyes and shrugs her shoulders.

"Then, today you wouldn't even pass Taylor the ball because of Zach *again*, causing us to almost lose the game. And don't forget that last week you got in a girl's face over Zach in the hallway after school. And then there was the Natasha incident in December. . . . We almost lost three games because of your suspension. What's with you, Kylie?"

Kylie crosses her arms. "Zach and I've been together for more than two years. It's different." She shoots me a look and I slide down farther in my seat.

"That's great, but we almost blew a game because of you and Zach. You guys broke up. It's over." Tamika paces. "Hey, I'm no saint. I found myself scanning the stands looking for Dwight during the first half. Believe me, I'm all for guys and having a good time. I'm just saying that I'm not giving up this season and my college dreams because of a bunch of boys." She grabs a red marker off the white board shelf and violently pops the cap off. "Friday's game is huge. We all know that the scouts from the SoCal Suns and a bunch of colleges will be there. It's a must win."

A bunch of us start to shift in our seats. Everyone is incredibly nervous about the game.

"Right. So, from this point forward, we need to change our attitudes, ladies." Tamika scans the room, looking each one of us in the eye. When she reaches me, my stomach drops.

Continuing, Tamika begins pacing back and forth. "Remember when Eva skipped a preseason practice to go to Telluride to hang out with her boyfriend? And what happened to him?" She stops and glares at Eva.

Eva drums her fingers on the desk. "Uh. . . . We broke up."

"Exactly." Tamika perches in the front of the room, poised and confident. "And you lost your starting position. Coach Jackson always says she never regretted a moment she spent playing a sport or hanging with her teammates. She only regretted the times she chose a guy over her team."

Everyone nods their heads in unison. Tamika has a point.

"That's why I think we should try a new approach." Tamika turns toward the whiteboard, grabs a red marker, and writes the words "No More Boys" in big letters.

Everyone's mouths drop wide open. Kylie and Missy freeze in their seats.

"That's right. No more guys until the season is over. That means no more fighting among ourselves about guys or freaking out over some dude." Tamika turns back to the board and writes her name on the board under the heading. Then she turns back to us. "Are we all in or what? No boys until the season is over."

Wait. What? I finally snagged Zach and I have to give up guys? I'm all for "team bonding" and stuff, but these girls have hung out with way more guys than I ever will. They just don't get it. This is my one chance to be with my one and only B-Dub soul mate.

"What the heck are we going to do if there are no guys?" Missy asks.

For once, she has a point.

Kylie chimes in. "Oh, you know, sit home at night and knit each other little I-heart-Beachwood-Academy-even-though-everyone-screws-me-over booties."

"Basketball," Tamika sternly responds. "This is serious, guys. Playoffs start a week from today. If we lose against Richland, we're screwed."

Kylie rolls her eyes. "That's so not gonna happen."

Tamika looks totally fed up by this point. "No, actually, it's definitely possible. We barely beat them in December." She takes a deep breath and calms herself down. "So, what do you guys think?"

"Like ball instead of boys?" Eva says.

"Sounds like a band," Kylie snaps.

"Ball before boys!" Missy pipes in. But then Kylie elbows her and her expression turns sheepish.

"Yeah," Jessica adds. "I like ball before boys!"

"How about three-B for a three-peat?" Eva lights up.

"Perfect!" Tamika spins around and erases "No More Boys" with her hand and writes "3B 4 a 3Peat." Turning back to us, she calls for the moment of truth, "Okay, so who's in?"

One by one, my teammates saunter up to the board and sign their names underneath. I hang back for a second.

Kylie walks up to the board and grins. "Whatever. I'm done with Zach."

Missy giggles. "Weren't you just canoodling in the corner of the gym with him?"

Urgh. Did she just say canoodling?

"We were, uh . . . saying good-bye." Kylie quickly scribbles her name.

"What about Valentine's Day? It's like two weeks away." Missy asks before snatching the marker from Kylie. "Can that be a bye-day?"

Tamika puts her hands on her hips. "Winning is about sacrifice. Are you in or are you out?"

Missy looks at Eva, then at me, and lets out a deep breath. "Fine." She hurriedly signs and snaps the cap back on in a huff.

Jessica grabs the marker, and I slink behind her. If the rest of my teammates are signing, I guess I am too. No way I'm drawing extra attention to myself.

The signing frenzy is interrupted by the sound of the door creaking open. Nick pokes his head into the classroom. "You guys hanging at the courts tonight?"

Tamika looks at us, then Nick. "Nope. We're busy."

Nick's face twists in disgust. "What?"

"Yeah. We're busy," Kylie says, holding three flawlessly manicured fingers in front of her mouth.

"Three-B," Tamika says.

"What the heck is three-B?" Nick asks.

"Secret." Jessica giggles.

"Your loss." Nick shuts the door.

"Nope, I think you're the loser," Tamika says.

We all break out into more giggles.

"I know. They totally are the losers. We always have a better record than them." Eva smiles, crosses her arms, and moves her head side-to-side in "no you didn't" style. "E-v-e-r-y season."

"Exactly!" Tamika purses her lips.

"Anyone up for some sushi to celebrate our unstoppable season?" Jessica asks. "I know this great place."

"Well, I guess I'm not doing anything tonight if we're doing this three-B thing." Kylie rolls her eyes. "So I'm in, but I need something more than sushi. Sushi tastes like air."

"I like sushi," Missy adds, taking a step away from Kylie for fear of punishment.

"Sushi it is. Are you coming, Taylor?" Tamika looks at me.

All eyes are on me. I pull my sleeves over my hands and

cringe. I should really see Hannah. She's completely freaking out about the fashion show and needs me for fittings. On the other hand, I should be happy they're including me after everything I did. Still, I can't ignore my best friend duties. "You know I'd love to, but I have to go over Hannah's. . . ."

Kylie raises one eyebrow. "Yeah, right."

"I mean, I could come for a minute or two, but I promised Han—"

"And you always have to do what Hannah wants?" Kylie interjects.

"Back off, Kylie. We all signed the three-B contract," Tamika comes to my defense. "Remember three-B for a three-peat." She holds up three fingers.

"True dat." Eva smiles and signals a three like a rapper.

"Who's in?" Tamika stands up by the desk and we all gather around her, placing our hands in the middle.

"On three. Three-B!"

twenty-three

"Taylor, what the heck happened during the game today?" my dad demands, resting his arm on the steering wheel as he drives me home after the 3B meeting.

My stomach twists. "I don't know."

"And what is going on with you and Mike Tyson?"

"Kylie," I whisper.

He yanks the steering wheel. "Do you know what would have happened to my career if I spent my time socializing and fighting with my teammates?"

You would have missed your spot with the NBA? No wait, that's my fault. "What?" I play along.

"I would have never played professionally in Europe. You have to play your game despite distractions. If you want to make it to the highest level, you have to focus."

I lean my head against the car window and stare out at the moving beach. I hate myself right now. I mean, the least I can do is show up. Tamika is right. No more boys. If I wasn't out with Zach, I would have played better today and my team wouldn't have fallen apart.

I pick my head up and face my dad. "I'm sorry."

"How about five miles before school tomorrow?" He looks at me again, then back at the road.

"Sounds good," I say. And I mean it.

"You play the way you prep."

"Yup."

He lets out a deep breath. "Taylor, you have talent. An enormous amount of basketball talent. And I just don't want to watch you throw it away and end up like . . ." He pauses.

I wish he would just say it. I wish he would just say "like me."

twenty-four

After telling me that he needs to run an errand at Walgreens, my dad drops me of at home. I run up the stairs and call out to my mom.

"Honey, I'm in the bathroom!" she yells in response.

"Are you feeling okay?" I ask.

"I'm fine," she shouts back.

I yell out, "Okay, glad to hear it!" and make a beeline for my room.

Once I'm sitting safely on my bed, I look up "fuzziness" and "rapid heartbeat" on my computer, in the hope of finding any reason—other than I'm dying from drama—that I could have been feeling all funky during today's game. Pretty soon all the medical mumbo jumbo starts to freak me out, so I decide to log in to see what's happening at Beachwood. Immediately, my screen is bombarded with buzz about 3B. Most of my team-mates have listed it as their status, and tons of people have commented. Plus, Eva even made us a little logo that a bunch of people posted as their profile pic. Looks like the guys' basketball team also took our logo and is claiming to have their "own" 3B. Lots of drama. I make a quick pic switch with the logo, spend a half hour commenting, and click over to Zach's page.

Sure enough, his status is back to "In a Relationship." (For a few moments there, I could swear that he had *no* relationship status listed.) But his wall posts are bare except for one from Kylie telling him to shove it. It's signed, 3B.

Oh, snap!

I'm about to sign off when I get a message from Hannah.

HANNAH MONTGOMERY:	Where r u?
TAYLOR THOMAS:	What?
HANNAH MONTGOMERY:	Fittings?
TAYLOR THOMAS:	Comin over in a sec. Lots of drama.
HANNAH MONTGOMERY:	???
TAYLOR THOMAS:	Zach's back in a rela?
HANNAH MONTGOMERY:	*checking page*
HANNAH MONTGOMERY:	It's u!!!!!
TAYLOR THOMAS:	No way.
HANNAH MONTGOMERY:	Whaz 3B?
TAYLOR THOMAS:	Tell u later.
HANNAH MONTGOMERY:	Urgh. . . . Well then tell me about Zach's tongue. LOL.
TAYLOR THOMAS:	☺
HANNAH MONTGOMERY:	Putting finishing touches on ur wardrobe. ur going to look fab. Come over ASAP.
TAYLOR THOMAS:	Leaving now.

I shut my Mac and run back down the stairs.

twenty-five

"Don't move," Hannah says, adding extra silk fabric to the back of an ivory dress. Make that a miniscule nightgown only my mom—in her *L.A. High* days—would wear.

"It doesn't fit," I say, sucking in my stomach.

"It will. It just needs some adjustments." Hannah pins extra fabric to the back.

"If by 'adjustments' you mean at least ten more inches of material." I look down to see where the dress falls. Answer: right at my butt cheeks.

"I'm not done with it. The dress is way too girly still. It needs some punk!"

"How about some pants?" I look down at the hem.

"You think this is bad. You should see the mini. Anyway, your legs always look amazing in shorts, even in those ugly mesh basketball ones."

"Mini?" I swallow a lump.

"Yeah. Remember I showed you the shearling piece that I stole from my sister's UGG bag at lunch?" Hannah pulls the dress a little tighter and digs a pin in.

"That tiny thing?"

"It's part of the mini design." Hannah snaps her fingers, in mock sorority style, and bobs her head side-to-side. "My best design ever."

For a minute, I picture that tiny piece of fabric. A mini? That's not enough fabric for a headband, let alone a mini.

Hannah finally releases me. "Break time!" She rolls me out of the dress, making me feel like a mummy being unraveled. "Okay. So, now, that I've given you some time. You *need* to tell me what three-B means. . . ."

I take a deep breath and pull my warm ups on. "It's really no big deal. Just a contract with my teammates."

"Like a 'you won't mess around with Zach' contract?" Hannah plops on her bed, sprawling the dress across her lap.

"Sort of."

I grab Hannah's MacBook and boot up. As I sit down on my bed, I notice her shaking her head. "What?" I ask.

"Kylie's such a brat. She made the team sign some lame contract because she's pissed Zach likes you?"

"Kylie's not a brat." I scan through the posts.

"Whatever. You're probably leaving Kylie a comment right now. Even after she carved 'skank' on your locker." Hannah pulls out a pin from the silk fabric and violently digs it back into the dress.

My face flushes. That's when I notice Vi's status update: "Hitting the Kogi BBQ truck with Matt. Craving kimchi quesadillas."

For some strange reason, my stomach does a little flip. *The two of them sure are hanging out a lot together lately.* Curious to see what Matt has to say about the ever-desirable Vi, I type his name into the search box. And . . . over twenty Matt Moore's in the Los Angeles area. I scan the results.

I look up at Hannah, who is busy threading her needle. "Did you know Matt Moore doesn't have a page?"

Hannah subconsciously moves the skateboard at the side of her bed back and forth with her feet. "Vi told me he doesn't even have a cell phone."

"Really?"

She shrugs her shoulders. "Didn't you know that? I mean, he's *your* partner." She pauses and looks at the computer screen, which is now filled with my comments under people's posts. "Wow, Tay, that's crazy. You have a severe case of P.P."

"What's P.P.?"

"People Pleasing. You need rehab or something."

"What are you talking about? Other people comment on mine too. It's totally normal." I lay back under the canopy.

"No, Tay, commenting sometimes when the mood strikes is normal. Commenting on everyone's posts? All the time? No matter what? That's just compulsive." Hannah lays the material down next to her. "Sometimes I wonder if you're bipolar."

"What?!?" I sit up.

"I mean, obviously you're not. But you have to admit that

you are a doormat at school and a total beast on the court. What's the deal?"

"I don't know. I don't sit around and analyze myself." I flip open the laptop again and am surprised to see that Nick left a post on my wall, "Wanna play bball at the courts?" Under him, Chris Phillips (*the* Chris Phillips), left another wall post: "Whatcha doing?" Two other guys from the basketball team, who I swear didn't even know my name before, sent me friend requests. And I got hearts from both Chris and Zach. *What the???*

Hannah catches my expression and thinks it's our conversation that's freaking me out. "Listen, Tay, I'm not saying you should analyze yourself. I just hate seeing girls like Kylie walk all over—"

"No, Banana, it's not that." I shut her laptop and my breathing starts to race. Again.

"What's up?"

I roll my shoulders back and calm my breathing. "It's just so strange. I got friend requests from two random guys from the basketball team. And Nick and Chris Phillips both want to hang out all of a sudden."

Hannah grins.

"What?" I ask, putting my hands on either side of me to steady myself.

"Your stock went up."

"What?"

"You hooked up with Zach and your stock went up."

"What are you talking about?" I ask, wondering if maybe they just want to play one-on-one with the tallest female center in the history of creation.

"Zach brought up your B-Dub stock. They want to hook up with you, Tay!" Hannah pulls a piece of thread tighter. "You know what? Zach is probably bragging about how amazing you are. And so they can't resist finding out for themselves!"

I look at her, my mouth agape.

"You have to admit, it makes sense," she insists.

"Well, if you're right, there's no way I'm jinxing it by putting an end to my People Pleaser-ness." I reopen her laptop and spend the next hour fulfilling my various "pay it forward" duties. Hannah can call me a P.P. all she wants. My pay-it-forward strategy is finally working—the last thing I should do right now is stop.

twenty-six

A few days later, I'm dragging after too many early morning runs, practices with my dad, Hannah fittings, and Zach-avoidance maneuvers. Considering our big game against Richland is tonight, this isn't good. How am I ever going to face Rodriguez and impress the scouts?

"Taylor."

I jump, grabbing the shoulder of the person who just talked to me. Fortunately, it turns out to be Hannah.

"Guess what?" Hannah pushes me up, helping me find my balance.

"Banana, you scared me!"

"Sorry about that, but the gossip I have is too good to worry about little things like scaring you."

I do another little jump. This time out of excitement.

"Zach and Kylie definitely broke up for good. It's all over school." Hannah grabs my hands and joins in on my jumping.

"Okay, but that doesn't mean anything. Does it?"

"No, it does. I'm telling you he's 'in a relationship' with you."

"Still, how do you know for sure?" I ask, realizing that there's no way Hannah is right about this one.

"Here, check it out." Hannah thrusts her iPhone at me.

I type in my username and password. As I closely watch the progress bar, my heart does some more of its new favorite activity—racing. Finally, my homepage appears, and I see the message I've been waiting for: "Please confirm that you're in a relationship with Zachary Murphy." I stare at the screen, dumbfounded. Oh. My. God.

"Let me see! Let me see!" Hannah calls out.

I pass her the phone, not saying a word.

Hannah takes one quick glance. "I was right! I knew it." She turns to me and adopts the *Miss Congeniality* sing-song voice, "You're in a relationship. With Zachary Murphy—"

"Banana, cut it out! Someone will hear you." I grab the phone back from her, log off, and put the screen on sleep mode. By "someone," I obviously mean Kylie.

"Who cares if they hear me? Let them! Because . . . *you're in a relationship. with Zachary Murphy.*" Continuing the *Miss Congeniality* voice, Hannah does a little dance.

"Hannah!"

"Okay, okay," Hannah says. Then she eyes my outfit. "What has gotten into you lately? You get visited by the magical clothes fairy?"

"What are you talking about? I'm wearing sneakers like always."

I look down at my outfit. Along with my sneakers,

which I'm only wearing because my feet still hurt from my recent heels escapade, I'm sporting skinny jeans and an oversized red sweater, a vintage piece from my mom's *L.A. High* wardrobe.

Hannah shakes her head. "Don't tell me you expected me not to notice your outfit is totally different from what you normally wear."

"I—"

"But, if you're going to try to reinvent your style, you should definitely keep me in the loop."

Reinvent my style? I just thought that this was the type of thing other people wear.

"I mean, I'm totally digging the eighties vibe." She looks me up and down again. "But you need to commit to one look."

"What?"

"Just go with either 'I just came back from the gym' or 'I'm so sexy in my heels.' Don't mesh." She shakes her head. "But, anyway, are you going to accept Zach's request?" She violently shakes my arm like she's trying to remove my shoulder from its socket.

On cue, Zach, Nick, and a few other guys from the basketball team walk by. "Hey, Taylor," they say in unison. Time seems to freeze as Zach grins at me like he's Lucas Till from Taylor Swift's "You Belong With Me" video.

Hannah and I dumbly wave at them as they pass us. I'm not sure which one of us is more in shock. Once they're out of earshot, Hannah lets out an "Ohmigod" in a single breath. Her eyes bug. "Now, you have to accept his request."

"Hannah!" Violet aggressively struts toward us, her minions trailing close behind. "Where are my black Manolos?" she screeches.

"I don't have your Manolos." Hannah flips her pale blond hair over her shoulder, turning her back to her sister.

Violet steps in between Hannah and me, placing her hands on her hips. "I know you have them."

"I don't have your stupid shoes."

"Hannah. . ." Violet whines. Behind her, her entourage fans out, surrounding us. "You are completely ruining my day." Violet huffs and continues to argue with Hannah.

I feel a tap on my shoulder and turn around. By habit I look down, but instead of looking at the top of someone's head (people should really pay attention to dandruff issues— tall people have front row access), I'm staring at the green alligator on Zach's black Lacoste shirt.

"Hey. I was wondering . . ." Zach says, scratching the tip of his square chin.

I stiffen up. I mean, two days ago, this was my dream. Seriously, I had a dream that Zachary Murphy was standing in front of me in this same hallway, asking me out. Except, in the dream I was taller than I am now (if that's humanly possible), my hair was chopped off like Eva from *America's Next Top Model* season three (Hannah's been TiVoing episodes for me to prepare for the fashion show), and I was waiting for a photo shoot, wearing white granny panties and a sports bra that made me look flatter than the Pacific Coast Highway.

"I was wondering if you want to hang out tonight." Zach leans against my locker and stares into my eyes.

Although my first inclination is to blurt out, "Yes, I will hang out with you and marry you and have your babies," I restrain myself. Unlike a basketball game, where there can only be one winner and one loser, this invite is far from clear-cut. If I say yes, I'll be violating 3B, causing my basketball career to suffer and my friends to hate me. If I say no, then I'll miss out on a once in a lifetime opportunity with a guy I've been mad crushing on. The only one guy who won't make me feel ridiculous because of my height.

"Sure, she'll go." Hannah wedges between Zach and me, waking me out of my Zach-induced trance.

"Uh, wait, I uh . . ." I stammer.

"I'll text you later." Zach turns around and walks down the hallway. Not a reaction. Not even a little smile. Guys like Zach are used to yeses.

Once Zach is far enough away, I let the freakage commence. "What are you *doing*? I can't hang out with Zach anymore!"

Hannah rolls her eyes. "You're telling me that you can't hang out with *the* Zachary Michael Murphy??? You've seriously gone off the deep end."

"No, you don't understand. Three-B," I whisper.

Hannah swipes the air. "They'll get over it. It's a stupid Kylie rule." Then, she swings her Vans bag over her shoulder. "I have a serious problem. I need more silk fabric. Do you think Vi will notice if I dice up another Versace dress?"

"Didn't she just ream you for taking her shoes?"

"Dude. That wasn't me. That was her being certifiable. Anyway, so about the fabric, I'm thinking. . . ."

As Hannah blabs on and on, I shut my locker and try to calm my trembling hands. This is so unfair. I finally somehow manage to snag Zach and I can't even hang out with him because my team decided to enact a rule. A rule for cool girls like Kylie and Missy who have their choice of boys. Not me. Gotta love Beachwood Academy.

twenty-seven

Why my so-called B-Dub stock went up:

1. The other guys on the b-ball team want to play one-on-one with me because I'm big.
2. Zach told Chris Phillips he can kiss me without objection because I'm seriously desperate.
3. My pay-it-forward strategy is working ☺
4. Zach told the guys in order to play one-on-one with my amazingly talented dad, they'll have to get through me first.
5. Zach is telling everyone how much fun we had together!!!!

"So, how's the new couple?" Matt rocks back on the rear legs of his silver chair.

"Who?" I act nonchalant, looking up from my list. "You and Vi?"

"You and Murph." He grins.

"Who told you?" I shut my notebook, realizing my virgin churn in the Beachwood rumor mill isn't all it's cracked up to be.

"Heard it around."

"No, really, who told you?" I lean toward him, catching a

whiff of something spicy like cinnamon. *When did Matt start smelling yummy?* I peek at his feet again. Still small.

"No one in particular," Matt says, playing with the strings on his Beachwood Lacrosse hoodie, the same hoodie he wears pretty much everyday.

"You okay?" Matt asks, showing off his deep dimples. I resist the urge to stick the eraser end of my pencil in his cheek canyons. Too cute.

"Yeah, I guess I'm just stressed," I say, flipping my pencil between my long fingers like a baton. "Been a long day and it's only fourth period."

"Shouldn't you be spreading the word about you and Murph? I figured you would want everyone to know about you guys since he's the man and all." Matt stretches his hands behind his head.

"Shouldn't you be choosing what party to attend tonight?" I decide to go for it and poke Matt with the eraser end of my pencil. He shrinks back, but I can't tell if he actually minds. "Anyway, I'm giving up guys for a while."

Matt chuckles.

"Wait. You think that's funny?" I sit back.

He laughs again.

"It's not funny." I cross my arms.

He grins and his cute canyons pop again. Dimples are my weakness. A few years back, it began with *Twilight*'s Kellan Lutz's, then it was Zach's solo crater, and now I can't help but notice Matt's. In fact, the more that I think about it, Matt kind of resembles Kellan Lutz.

"What?" I ask, forcing myself to concentrate on the conversation.

He looks at the ceiling. Then his chocolate M&M eyes meet mine. "Do you like Zach?"

"Sure. I mean, he's an athlete and he's as tall as—" I pause wondering if Matt's sensitive about his height handicap.

Matt isn't shaken. Nothing shakes Matt. Not a lacrosse championship game or a scholarship or a fight on the field. Or even Beachwood Academy . . .

"Then, if you like him, go for it." He shrugs.

"It's not that simple." I chew on my bottom lip.

Matt shakes his head and smiles. I recently noticed that Matt smiles a lot. "Why?"

"We're doing this three-B for a three-peat thing."

"What's the heck is three-B?" He pops a piece of Big Red gum in his mouth.

"Ball before boys for a three-peat." I grin proudly. "Don't you guys ever do anything like this? You know, make a pact to give up distractions for a season?"

"That stuff never comes before sports."

I roll my eyes. "Whatever. Weren't you at the football game last fall when Nick Solerno and Matt Connelly gave each other a serious pounding after the game?"

"That's football. Those guys are tools." Matt grins. "I

just don't let outside problems get in the way of my game. I have a lot riding on lacrosse." He looks down, suddenly serious.

I think about asking what he means by that, but instead decide to switch topics, since he looks so sad. "Hey, did you write any more poems?"

"Nope. Been busy." He yanks his sweatshirt sleeves to his elbows, exposing a huge pale pink scar on his forearm.

"What's that?" I ask, pointing at the scar. "It's huge."

He peeks at the puffy scar and pulls his sweatshirt sleeves back down to his wrists. "Nothing."

"Did you get it from lacrosse or something?"

"Yeah. Lacrosse." Matt's eyes stay downcast.

I gotta get him out of this funk. "Can I see some of your old stuff?" I reach under his English books for his black leather notebook, causing his Beachwood planner to fall on the floor. I lean over to pick up the open planner and notice tomorrow's date circled, along with the entry, "Doctor with Dad, 4 p.m." *What the heck?!?* The appointment below it then catches my attention: "Violet, 6 p.m., 555-9176." All of a sudden, my palms feel sweaty.

Matt pulls the planner out of my hand and gives me a look like I violated his trust. *All I wanted to do was help. . . . I didn't mean to . . .*

"Okay, class. Return to your seats. Word-of-the-Day time is over," Mr. Ludwig yells above the classroom din.

As Mr. Ludwig resumes his usual droning, I stare straight

ahead at the whiteboard, wondering what's really going on with Matt.

What's wrong with his dad? Did his family used to live in Beverly Hills? Does he now carry a free lunch ticket because his parents can't even afford to feed him? Does he travel on three buses everyday for two hours from downtown L.A. just to get to Beachwood so he can play on the lacrosse team? If so, what the heck happened?

But more than anything, I keep coming back to one question: *Why oh why is he messing with Tornado Violet?*

twenty-eight

"Hey." Zach stops by my locker after school. "So, where do you want to hang out tonight? The movies? Santa Monica? We could grab something at In-N-Out Burger."

I take a deep breath. Zach is even more uber-tempting (if that's possible) when he's dangling In-N-Out Burger in front of me. But I have to say no. I don't have a choice.

"I don't know if that's such a great idea." I cautiously look around to see if any of my teammates are within sight distance. I'm dead if anyone spots me with Zach.

Zach continues to talk. "Why? Because of the three-B thing?" He rolls his eyes. "Let me guess, it was Kylie's idea."

"No, but I—"

"I'll text you around seven after practice?"

"Uh. Really. I shouldn't—" I try to interject.

Zach winks and walks away before I can say anything else.

A few seconds later, Chris Phillips walks up to my locker. "You busy, Tay?"

"Nope," I say, staring into my locker in an attempt to figure out what I have to bring home today. Between all this Zach attention, helping Hannah out with her designs, my anxiety about the upcoming Richland game, and geometry time with Jessica, I can't even remember what I have for homework.

"I was wondering . . ." Chris begins.

I struggle to distract myself from Chris's all-consuming hotness. *English: Word of the Day and critical essay. Need notebook and* Catcher in the Rye. *Check. History: Read chapters seven and eight. Need textbook. Check. Do I have math?*

"Do you want to hang out after practice?"

Yeah, I definitely have math homework. *Wait a second.* What?!? *Did Chris Phillips just ask me to hang out?* I turn to face him. "What did you just say?"

"I said, do you want to hang out after practice?"

"Wait, what?" *Did Christopher Phillips, the freaking senior homecoming king, just ask me to hang out?*

"Maybe you should get your ears checked, Tay. What I wanted to know is if you want to hang out after practice?" He leans against my locker.

I stare down into Chris's baby blues and think that I must have fallen asleep in class and woken up in an alternate universe, one where it's normal for Taylor Thomas, the towering giraffe who spends her time pleasing people for fear of being disliked, is suddenly catapulted to ultra-hotties-love-her land. I shake myself. This is Beachwood. Not Oz. And I'm a member of the basketball team, first and foremost. "Ah. Chris, I don't know."

"Great. I'll catch up with you later."

What's with cuties not taking no for an answer?

twenty-nine

"Who wants brand new three-B tanks from American Apparel?" Eva charges into Richland's locker room, holding up a large shopping bag.

I'm staring at my locker, attempting deep yoga breaths. This is it. Today is do or die. When the scout from the SoCal Suns picks me over Rodriguez for the center spot, the doors to California basketball heaven open up to me. And Dad can finally rest assured that giving up basketball was worth it.

"This is exactly what I needed to help me cope with the number of scouts here today." Tamika pulls a tank out of the bag and shakes it out.

"Yeah, me too," Kylie says, rolling her eyes.

"Be glad your entire future isn't riding on this game," Tamika says, whipping Kylie with her tank.

"Believe me, Captain T." Kylie grabs a tank and whips her back. "My time will come this spring on the softball field."

"Come on, Tamika, you're going to do fab," Missy says, pulling her straight platinum hair up into a high ponytail. Leave it to Missy to always look her best. Even if it's on the basketball court.

I grab a tank for myself. "Love it. Can't believe you got them to make these so quickly. Thanks, Eva."

"I figured we could wear the tanks under our jerseys today," Eva says, squishing the shopping bag down now that all the shirts have been taken. "You know to remind everyone that although today is all about the scouts, we're also a team."

"Good stuff, Eva," Jessica says, pulling her tank over her sports bra. "Fits perfectly."

"You're right, Eva. This game means more than the scouts. This is a *must win* game if we want to three-peat." Tamika is suddenly serious. "If we lose, we have to pray for a tie for the conference and a rematch. And the last thing I want to do is have to rely on maybes."

"Yeah," I say, letting out a deep breath. I rub the soft cotton fabric of the tank in between my fingers for extra good luck.

"Hey. Where are Zoe and Abby?" Kylie asks, looking around.

"They're at the JV game," Tamika answers.

"Too bad. I guess it's just you, Taylor. Did we ever initiate Taylor properly to the team?" Kylie looks up at me.

"Do you really think ten minutes before beginning our warm-up for the Richland game is the best time?' Tamika raises her left eyebrow.

"Total stress release." Kylie smiles mischievously. "Shaving cream or the shower?"

I slink toward the door.

"She'll be too wet to play if we toss her in the shower," Missy adds.

"Then, shaving cream it is!" Kylie pulls four bottles of shaving cream out of her bag (somebody planned ahead) and Tamika grabs my waist.

Pretty soon, white blobs are flying all over the locker room. It doesn't take long for me to lose count of how many times my face gets smashed with a towel pie. For a second, I allow myself to dream that this is the revenge that Kylie had planned all along. I mean, it's a few minutes before I'm supposed to go out on the court for one of the most important games of my life, and I'm completely covered in shaving cream. *What else could she possibly do to me?*

Just then, I double over as my stomach gets hit with an assault of shaving cream. I look up and see Kylie, staring at me with a smirk on her face and a glint in her eyes. That's when I realize: *This isn't over.*

thirty

"All set." The ref stands between me and Nikki Rodriguez. She's taller than the last time we met and, if possible, even more imposing. *This is gonna be fun.*

Rodriguez snarls at me. I nod back at her, remove the last remaining bit of shaving cream from my hair, and quickly glance over at my dad. He's on the edge of his seat, staring out at the court. Seated to his right is the SoCal Suns coach. She's dressed in a purple jacket with a tiny yellow sun.

Then I bring my focus back to the court. Time to concentrate on the only thing that matters at this moment: the orange ball.

The ref points to us and looks at the clock table. "Ready," he says. Then, he tosses the ball into the air. Rodriguez gets to it first, reaches up, and taps it back to her guard.

"Four," the Richland guard shouts, holding up four fingers.

Rodriguez sprints behind me. The Richland guard fires the ball to her before I realize what she's doing. Rodriguez easily lays up the ball.

"Get in the game, Taylor! Come on!" Coach Jackson screams from the sideline.

As Rodriguez passes me, she sneers. "It's all mine." Then she nods at the SoCal Suns coach.

I take off, finding my spot underneath the basket, and shove Rodriguez for position.

Kylie dribbles down the court. "Wildcat Two!" she screams.

Good. This is my play. I'll show the SoCal Suns coach what I've got. I sprint toward the foul line with my hands up. Kylie looks at me, as if she's considering passing the ball, but then turns abruptly and fires the ball to Tamika.

Wait. This isn't a Wildcat Two. I cut for position. With Rodriguez on my tail, it's almost impossible to break free. I look to Kylie for a pick. She turns her head. *What the heck?* She's supposed to pick for me. Guess the whole shaving cream fiasco wasn't her version of adequate revenge after all.

Tamika sets up for a jump shot, but Rodriguez manages to block it. Then she grabs her own rebound and takes off.

As I sprint down the court, I look at the Suns scout as she furiously scribbles notes. *Please, please, pick me.*

As the game progresses, Kylie continues to ignore me. Unfortunately, unlike last time, Coach doesn't notice (and Coach Martie's too busy flipping through the play binder). Like everyone else, she just thinks that Rodriguez must be playing amazing defense. And that's not to say that she isn't. But that's definitely not the whole story.

Eventually, I become frustrated, play sloppy, and foul-out

late in the third quarter. I take a seat on the bench and watch as the seconds tick away. Now, with seven seconds left, we're getting slaughtered by Richland 42–30. And there's nothing I can do about it.

To pass the time, I make a mental list of reasons why this situation blows:

1. I'm warming the bench, unable to prove to anyone that Kylie screwed me over. Big time.
2. I am going to lose the center spot on the SoCal Suns to Rodriguez, who is going to rub it in my face like crazy.
3. If Richland beats us, we won't get to walk away with the playoff spot.
4. Hopefully, we'll play Richland again for the three-peat next week
5. I really don't want to see Rodriguez ever again.
6. Kylie is ruining my life.

The buzzer rings, and the Richland players run to center court, yelling, "We did it! 42–30 baby!"

Then—the icing on the cake—the SoCal Suns coach approaches Rodriguez.

I promptly bury my face in a towel. Just then, I feel a tap on my back. Coach Martie sits next to me. "You okay?"

I shake my head and bury it again.

"Remember, everything happens for a reason." She pauses.

I keep my head in my towel, wiping away the tears that are beginning to form.

Martie continues, "During my sophomore year, I was approached to play soccer overseas for the summer. I was so nervous, I couldn't sleep a wink the entire week before the scout was coming to watch me play. Of course, I ended up hugely stinking up the tryout."

I lift my head a second but Martie's fuzzy.

"Later that summer, I got really lucky. One girl from another club team dropped out, so I was offered a second tryout. This time I made a vow to remember that soccer is supposed to be fun. I decided to go out there and do my best, but not to think of that one game as the end-all, be-all. And sure enough, I made the team. It turned out to be the best thing that could have happened because I got to play with my sister for two seasons. As you know, five years later she was killed in an accident." Martie's voice cracks. "I wouldn't give up that time with her for anything."

A shiver runs up my spine. "Coach, I'm so—"

"No need to say anything." Martie clears her throat. "I just want you to remember what's important. That's all." She pauses, wiping away a tear that escaped. "Just promise me you'll think about what I'm saying."

I look Martie directly in the eyes. "Sure, Coach."

"Thanks, Taylor. I know you'll do the right thing." Martie gives my shoulder a squeeze and walks away.

Martie is right. I think about confronting Kylie. But that wouldn't be what's best for the team.

A few minutes later, I take a deep breath and run up the bleachers to tell my dad that I need to talk to Tamika before I can meet him outside. Time to put my pay-it-forward plan back into effect.

"Congrats!" I exclaim upon reaching Tamika. "I know we didn't win, but eighteen points, twelve assists, and ten rebounds—way to step it up!" I muster the strength for a huge smile.

She beams back at me. "A coach from USC said he'd be in touch!" She grabs my hands and jumps up and down. "Can you believe it? I thought for sure I had no shot since I'm a senior. But, he said I've been on USC's radar since last year."

"Are you kidding? Of course I can believe it. You're amazing!" I give a little clap in her honor.

"Sorry about the Suns," she says, tilting her head. "Between Rodriguez getting the center spot and our having to play Richland again for a do-or-die division playoff when we could have ended everything tonight . . . it's all kind of bittersweet."

"Don't worry about it. We'll kill Richland next time we face them." I fake a smile. "And you better believe that I'm seriously going to bring my A-game."

"Oh, I know you will! Because Coach just told me we're playing Richland next Saturday. Our teams have matching records so we have to play a one-game playoff to settle the

Head
GAMES

conference tie." Tamika hugs me and dashes off to go share the good news with the other members of the team.

I'm about to run into the locker room for a quick shower when I hear "Hi, Taylor." A woman about an inch taller than me extends her hand.

I shake it, and again take in the sun logo in the top right-hand corner of her purple jacket.

"I'm Coach Delamarte from the Southern California Suns."

"Yes, of course. Nice to meet you." I bravely smile.

"I just wanted to let you know that although we decided to go with Rodriguez this season, we would love for you to try out—"

Yay. Another shot! She knows I can do better than I did today. My pay it forward method never fails.

"For the B team."

"The B team?" I ask, confused.

"Yup, the B team. You should be proud of yourself. This is a big accomplishment for a freshman. That said, there will be loads of competition for the center spot, so I can't guarantee anything, but I think if you step up your game, you just might earn a spot to play behind another star freshman, Rodriguez."

I nod my head. "Sounds great. Thanks," I say through clenched teeth. I guess a B team offer is better than nothing, but still, I can't help but wonder: *Is B for bad?*

thirty-one

I hole myself up all weekend after the Friday night debacle. The only time I leave my room is to work out with my dad, and even that becomes a struggle when he informs me that Coach Delamarte told him that she'd still love to have me play for the "real" Suns someday after my game matures. In light of that revelation, one that provokes a steady stream of tears, I refuse to speak to anyone outside of my family other than Hannah. On the bright side, by never leaving my house, I avoid any guy temptations. And as I never responded to Zach's relationship request, I guess that means that technically I'm still a 3B member in good standing. When Monday rolls around, I put my best face forward. After school my efforts to remain upbeat are challenged when Coach Martie meets us in the gym and announces, "Follow me to the beach. Team building today!"

"Joy," Kylie says.

As much as Kylie and I aren't on good terms right now, I'm tempted to echo her sentiment.

We run, more like sprint, the three blocks to the beach.

By the time we arrive, we're huffing and puffing. With national team soccer alumna Martie leading the pack, we quickly discover that our regular cardio workouts just aren't cutting it.

The waves spray white mist onto the sand and the sun warms our backs. I breathe in the pungent smell of salt, attempting to deflect hyperventilation. No wonder I tanked the tryout. I bet Rodriguez would nail this run in under five minutes.

Martie, not at all out of breath, unzips her backpack and pulls out eight bandanas.

"What kind of team building stuff are we doing?" Tamika asks, with one hand on her hip.

Like Tamika, the other upperclassmen are all a bit skeptical about team-building exercises. Apparently, their distaste for team building originated a year ago in gym class when Mr. Gibbs, one of our phys. ed. teachers, made them climb trees, and Eva fell off a branch after her partner miscalculated whether it would hold her weight. She ended up breaking two bones in her foot and spending the night in the ER. Plus, she missed the remainder of the basketball season. Naturally, this event didn't exactly engender good will toward team building.

Coach Martie shouts over the sound of the crashing waves. "As you guys know, after the last two games, Coach Jackson and I expressed our concern about the team." She holds up a royal blue bandana, and we all shift uncomfortably.

What could she possibly have planned for us? "So, we decided to do a team-building activity I did with my soccer players a few years ago that really helped bring the team together."

Martie continues. "After I assign partners, you're going to tie a bandana around your partner's eyes. You'll notice that there are seashells hidden between the perimeter of the four red flags on the beach." In unison we look around and spot the four red flags and the scattered seashells. "One seashell has your partner's name on it. You must guide your blind partner to the seashell with her name on it and help her pick it up."

We scan the area, attempting to find our seashells. Jessica inches toward one peeking out of the sand showing the letter J.

"But, here's the catch. You cannot touch your partner. You can only guide her with words."

"Sounds like a game show," Tamika pipes up.

Martie nods. "Okay, here are the partners. The first person I call out is the guide. The second person is the blindfolded shell-seeker." She looks down at a card. "Tamika and Jessica." Jessica darts toward Tamika and they grab a bandana. "Zoe and Abby." Zoe and Abby look at each other and smile. "Eva and Missy." Missy claps, jogging over toward Eva. I survey the group and gulp.

"And Kylie and Taylor."

thirty-two

Before I can grab the turquoise bandana, Kylie snatches it and rolls her eyes at me. She inches up behind me. Standing on her tippy-toes, she wraps the bandana around my eyes. I'm about to move away when she knots and yanks it behind my head. Then, she yanks it again and again.

"Stop. It's tight enough!" I say, feeling the stiff fabric dig into the back of my scalp.

"Nope. I think you need one more pull." She tugs and lets out a soft grunt.

I smack Kylie's hands away.

"Okay!" Martie yells. "Begin on my whistle. The first partners who find their shell are excused from the upcoming mile-and-a-half run."

Martie whistles.

"Left!" Kylie shouts.

I take a step.

"No, right!" she screams.

As I begin to turn, I feel another arm brush by me. I

wonder if Kylie would tell me if anyone was about to run into me. *Probably not.*

"Okay, straight," she declares.

I stretch out my arms, trying to feel for someone or something just in case. Then I take a few uneasy steps before tripping ever so slightly.

"Come on, Taylor," Kylie whines. "I know you're super into inflicting pain and suffering, but I'm so not in the mood to do a beach run today."

Again, I stumble a bit on a clump of sand. "Who is?"

"Pay attention. We don't have time for falls," she snaps.

"Kylie, I'm not planning on falling," I reply. I'm trying to be as nice as possible to Kylie, but I can't take much more of this.

"Whatever," Kylie says.

Guess she's out of comebacks.

"Oh wait, Taylor, there's your name on the shell, there." Her voice moves in front of me. "Carefully, move toward the sound of my voice. Walk a little to the right."

I take a step toward the right.

"Too much. Just a little bit. Not that much."

I stop.

"No keep moving."

No wonder Zach breaks up with her so much. She's beyond annoying.

"Okay, just three more tiny steps."

I take one, two, three steps, then stop.

"Bend down, gently."

I kneel down on my knees and start feeling for the shell.

"That's it. A little to the right."

I feel around in the sand until I touch something hard and smooth. Carefully, I pick it up.

"Coach, we got it!" Kylie shouts.

I tug at my bandana. It won't budge. I tug on it again. Nothing. Then I feel someone loosening it for me. When the bandana falls away from my eyes, I see Martie standing there, grinning at me. She takes the shell from my hands, and sure enough, my name is written out in uppercase letters.

Martie turns toward the group. "Kylie and Taylor were the first to retrieve their seashell. They win," she announces.

"I knew you were quite the feeler." Kylie elbows me.

"And you're quite the b—uh, br . . . illiant guide," I force myself to cough out the words and elbow her back harder.

"Everybody else, please help your partners take off their bandanas and form a circle," Martie instructs us.

"Aren't we done yet?" Missy groans.

"You can always join the JV squad." Coach Martie raises her eyebrows at Missy. "Remember, there are plenty of younger girls ready and willing to take a senior's spot for next year. And who would be more than happy to join our team-building activities."

"Team building rocks!" Missy grins and pumps her fist.

"Yeah, I kind of like it too," I add.

All at once, my teammates look at me, their mouths

open in surprise. It's rare that I contribute to group discussions.

"Okay, so on to the next activity." Martie hands each of us a card and pen. "This time, you're going to write two truths and a lie. For example, if I were writing a card, I might write, I played for the U.S. National soccer team, my middle name is Jane, and I hold the Beachwood Academy record for most goals scored in women's soccer." She looks around. "Does anyone know the lie?"

"Your middle name is Joan." Tamika waves her hand. "Not Jane."

"Exactly. See, this shows that Tamika really knows me." Coach Martie smiles. "So, everybody get to work. And when you're done, hand your cards back to me. I'm going to read them aloud and your teammates will have to guess who wrote each card and which line is the lie."

I stare at the blank card in my hand. *What the heck am I going to write?* That I'm a closet cyber stalker/addict? That my mom is a former TV actress? That I blew the SoCal Suns tryout because of boys and Kylie? Or that I'm scared to death to walk the catwalk on Friday night?

I notice that most of the girls start scribbling right away, though a few randomly look around, clearly confused about what to write.

Finally, with a shaky hand I write my first truth.

1. Basketball is my life.

thirty-three

Ten minutes later, the team re-groups and Martie collects the cards.

"First one." As she pulls out a card, I sift my hands through the sand, watching the tiny, tan particles fall. Although I didn't write anything incriminating, this whole thing makes me feel weird.

Martie begins reading aloud. "I love Ben and Jerry's Chocolate Chip Cookie Dough ice cream. My uncle's name is George Clooney, but he's not the famous one. Last year, during a Hawaiian vacation, I hula danced in front of a huge crowd."

"Missy," Kylie declares, rolling her eyes. "This so lame. The lie is the chocolate chip cookie dough."

"Seriously? George Clooney?" Tamika asks.

"Yup." Missy grins. "Kylie is right. All true, except I love brownie batter."

"Next one." Coach Martie smiles. "This one says: My favorite sport is basketball. I once met Fergie. I'm the lead singer of a band."

My teammates look around.

"Has to be Eva." Missy says.

"Yup." She smiles proudly.

"Is the band the lie?" Kylie asks.

"Nope. Just started one with a couple of friends." Eva laughs. "Never met Fergie."

Martie continues. "This one says: Basketball is my life. My dad played for the NBA. And my favorite color is blue."

My stomach twists.

"Abby?" Tamika suggests.

Abby shakes her head no.

"Taylor?" Missy asks.

My teammates look at me, and I nod.

"Oh, duh, I remember you telling me that your dad never actually played for the NBA," Kylie says, rolling her eyes and silently stage laughing at me when Martie isn't looking.

Of course, it had to be Kylie who figured out the lie. And to be so mean about it. *When is she going to let the Zach thing go?* I mean, the two of them broke up.

Martie resumes reading. "My first kiss was behind a cliff when I was eleven. In-N-Out Burger is my fave. I love basketball, but softball is my number one passion."

"Kylie," Missy and Tamika say at the same time.

"And In-N-Out Burger is Zach's fave, not hers." Missy adds.

Kylie sits up straighter.

That's right. Zach and I both love In-N-Out Burger, unlike Kylie. We're totally meant to be soul mates. As soon as the season wraps up and 3B disbands, I will find a way to win a spot on the Suns, and Zach and I will live happily ever after, eating In-N-Out Burger together for all eternity.

thirty-four

We end with musical hacky sack. Five minutes into the game, and only Martie and Eva remain. Seven taps back and forth later, Eva loses, after getting distracted by the sudden silence of Martie's ancient boom box.

Martie raises her hands in victory. "And I was looking forward to running today!" She beams. "Guess it's up to you girls."

"What's up with the retro eighties boom box?" Kylie makes a dig at Martie.

"Wouldn't you like to know. . . . Only so many of us can have such sophisticated taste." Martie pulls a stopwatch out of her bag. "Anyway, girls, it's time for beach runs." She hands Kylie her stopwatch. "As promised, you and Taylor will time them." Turning to the team, she says. "The rest of you, run down to Malibu Colony, then back. Run it in less than twelve minutes or repeat the run. And if you have to repeat, Taylor and Kylie will have to join you." Martie picks up the boom box. Jessica and I help Martie gather her bag of bandanas and cards.

Kylie glares at our teammates. "Keep it under twelve."

"And when you're done, you have one last activity to

finish before you can call it a day." Martie stops at the dunes and grabs her bag from Jessica and me. "During the walk back to Beachwood, I want you each to use one word to describe each other. The rules are to keep it positive and mention at least one new trait per teammate."

We all look around, thinking the same thing: *That's a lot of traits to come up with.*

"Got it?" Martie smiles.

"Got it," Tamika says.

"After that, you guys are free to shoot around or do whatever it is you have to do. We'll have a regular practice tomorrow after school to prepare for Saturday's game against Richland. And let's make this game one they'll never forget."

We nod in unison and someone shouts, "Yeah, Wildcats!"

"That's the spirit! Okay, so to recap—first you run, then you describe your teammates, and then you're free to shoot around. Don't let me find out that any of those steps went overlooked. Remember, we really need to come at Richland with everything we've got, and to do that, we have to work together. Sound good?" Martie gives us all a once over, and then yells, "See you later!" as she takes off running back toward school.

With Martie out of earshot, Jessica turns to me. "You know, she's really sweet."

I nod back at her. "Yeah, I agree. I really like having her around."

Abby hears us and joins in. "Oh, me too. I didn't think I was going to, but her optimism is contagious."

"Def," says Zoe, doing some lunges in preparation for the run.

Kylie holds up the stopwatch. "Okay, girls, let's get a move on it. I don't have all day!"

My teammates begin sprinting down the beach toward Malibu Colony, leaving Kylie and me behind. Kylie falls into a seated position, looking kind of sad, and starts drawing her name in the wet sand with her finger.

I shut my eyes, practice my footwork, and begin to move my feet as if I'm Candace Parker inside the paint.

I'm so going to dunk by junior year.

"Hey," a voice bellows as I'm about to pretend dunk. I jump.

Matt Moore walks toward me from behind the dune grass. *Where did he come from?*

"You scared me," I say, holding my hand to my chest. "Were you watching us or something?"

"I'm always watching you." He grins, but I don't take it seriously because Matt says flirty stuff like this to everyone.

"What are you doing here?" I ask.

"I'm coming back from the gym." Matt digs his hands in his shorts, which show off his thick, cut legs. He shrugs his shoulders, moving his hoodie toward his ears. He looks extra snuggly, like a warm teddy bear. I resist the urge to hug him. Not like a boyfriend-girlfriend hug (because he's too short and I might crush him), more like a stuffed animal hug before drifting off to sleep.

"Where's Vi?"

Matt adjusts his Beachwood Academy lacrosse bag over his shoulder. "How should I know?" He looks around. "Where's Murph?"

I snap my head around toward Kylie. "Beats me."

He looks down and kicks some sand around.

It's strange, but for the first time, I feel kind of weird around Matt. I can't figure it out. I mean, we hang out in English together every day. Not knowing what to say, I opt for the same question I went for the last time we were together: "Did you write any more poetry?"

"Shhhh . . ." He looks up at me with his big, deep brown eyes and inches closer. So close I have to look down. "Remember that's our secret." His hot breath hits my neck, and out of nowhere I feel a tingly sensation bottle up inside.

Wait, what? I've only ever thought of Matt as puppy dog cute, but right now, he's definitely hitting Kellan Lutz status once again (except Matt's more of a Nick Jonas than a Kellan, since Nick's also kind of short). Suddenly, it hits me: *Why am I even thinking this?* I take a step backward. "I better go. My teammates should be coming back from their run soon."

"Yeah, me too." Matt lets out a deep breath. "See you around."

"Yeah, see you around."

I watch Matt continue in the opposite direction of my teammates. Man, his butt looks good in his jeans. Maybe even better than Jonas's and Lutz's.

thirty-five

"Get 'em!" Out of nowhere, the guys' basketball team sprints across the sand and attacks us one by one. My teammates, just back from their beach run, attempt to escape by dashing toward the cliffs.

Dwight grabs Eva and swings her over his shoulder, running toward the surf. Zach scoops me up like a newlywed and steps in line behind Dwight. Nick chases Kylie. Jason grabs Jessica. Chris flips Tamika over his shoulder. Andrew grabs Missy. Zoe and Abby take off toward the dune grass.

"Let us go!" Eva yells.

"The water is frigid!" Tamika screams.

One by one the guys toss my teammates into the shimmering waves. Instead of chucking me into the ocean like the others, Zach drags me away from the group and plants a kiss on my lips before I can turn my head. Shivers run up my spine. And it's not just from the cool water splashing at our feet.

I glimpse at my teammates who are busy wrestling with the guys. In fact, Kylie has Nick in one of her infamous headlocks, compulsively checking behind her for a certain special someone. For a second, I wonder if she's ever choked that someone—eh, Zach.

"How about you meet up with me at the beach courts later?" Zach asks, out of breath.

Behind him, Jessica is wiggling away from Jason, whose lips are puckered up.

"I so want to, Zach, but I can't," I tell him.

"Blowing me off again, huh? I get it. Just say the word and I'll leave you alone."

"No, that's not it. It's not that I don't want to hang out, believe me. It's just—"

"Good. Because I'm not giving up on you." He pulls me so close that we're nose to nose.

Out of the corner of my eye, I spot my teammates emerging from the water.

"I gotta go," I say.

"I'll text you later," Zach whispers in my ear, sending tingles down my back. Gently, he releases me.

"Where are you going?" Nick calls.

Kylie flips her head upside down and gathers her blonde hair in a saturated ponytail on top of her head. "We're busy."

"Yeah," Missy shouts over the surf. "We have three things to do."

"Are you guys still doing that dumb three-B thing?" Nick taunts.

"You should give it a try. Maybe you guys would win a game or two," Kylie snickers. "Or three."

"Maybe we already are," Nick says.

That's when Jason jabs his arm. "Dude!"

thirty-six

We gather up our things from the beach. I linger for a bit, secretly admiring Zach as he strides into the water to join the guys in all his muscley glory. Yum.

"Come on, Skank," Kylie says jokingly and pulls me by my arm a little harder than necessary. At least, I think she's joking.

I follow my teammates, wistfully casting one glance back at Zach. It's as if I'm in a room full of fluffy white birthday cake and I'm not allowed to eat any.

"Losers," Kylie adds. She stops to double knot her sneakers. "When we're done with three-B, I'm going to start hanging out with college *men*. No more B-Dub *boys* for me."

"They're totally trying to mess with us," Eva says. "Jason was trying to kiss me. And it seems like it was just because he saw our three-B posts. What a tool."

"The whole thing is kind of weird, you know. All of a sudden, all these guys are asking me out. And before three-B, it was like crickets," Tamika says.

"Yeah, I know what you mean." Missy pipes up. "Chris Phillips and Andrew asked me to hang out today after practice. Though I guess it's kind of different for them to be asking *me*," she pauses, looking around at the rest of us, "as opposed to, uh—"

"Us too," Abby adds, nodding in Zoe's direction. Guess she chose to ignore Missy's dig.

I think back to Zach, and how Chris and a couple other guys messaged me out of the blue. *Was it only because of three-B?* Like some sort of twisted joke to see if I'd give in?

Kylie rolls her eyes.

Tamika shakes her head. "And I thought Dwight and Darren were just being nice."

"Losers," Kylie says.

"Resist, girls. We must resist." Tamika laughs. "They're just trying to throw us off our game."

"Resistance." Eva begins to dance to a silent beat.

Ughh. Eva has had five boyfriends already. Tamika has had three. Me, zero. One knee kiss and some tongue action. Speaking of resistance, I resist the urge to tell them: *Speak for yourself. I'm liking the attention.*

"Well, let's get this positive affirmation thingy over with. Who's up for Sprinkles?" Tamika picks up her bag.

"Sounds good to me," Missy answers. "The only way I'm going to swallow all of your compliments is if I have some cupcakes to sweeten my mood."

"What the?!?" Kylie trips over a leftover sneaker from the guys' pile of duds and falls arms outstretched into the sand.

Gotta love karma.

"Someone's excited about Sprinkles." Missy walks over to Kylie and helps her to her feet. Then Missy freezes. "Wait, what is this?"

She takes a few steps backwards, bends down, picks up a crumpled piece of paper next to the sneaker, and smoothes it with her hand. Her eyes widen. "Ohmigod." She holds the paper out to us.

"What?" Tamika grabs it, and we crowd around her.

3B—BABES, BASES, AND BASKETBALL

5   points—first base

10 points—second base

15 points—third base

20 points—homerun

5   point bonus for never been kissed

Points:

Nick—15 (Brooke, Stacy)

Zach—35 (Taylor★, Kylie, Annie★)

Jose—20 (Natasha, Eva, Violet)

Dwight—5 (Tamika)

Matt—30 (Violet, Natasha, Beatrice)

Chris—25 (Corrine, Brooke, Jessica★)

Jason—10 (Nicole★)

Andrew—20 (Brooke, Missy)

★—*Bonus Babes*

Head **GAMES**

"Uh-huh-uh-huh-uh . . ." I can't catch my breath. "Zach . . . and Matt???"

"Taylor, are you okay?" Jessica asks, her eyes full of concern. Everyone turns to look at me. I force myself to get my breathing under control and nod that I'm all right.

"I'm going to kill them," Tamika growls.

"They must suffer," Eva screeches.

"I think I'm going to be sick," Missy adds. "Brooke?"

My heart pounds so loudly in my chest that, for a second, I can't make out their conversation. All I can think is: *It was all a lie. It was all a lie. It was all a lie.* I actually believed those guys liked me, if only for a millisecond. There were just so many messages and texts, guys coming out of nowhere, begging to hang out with me. And now it turns out that all that matters to them is that I'm worth more points in this stupid, perverted game they're playing.

Think positive thoughts. I rub my temples and attempt to concentrate on what my teammates are saying.

Kylie grabs the paper and shreds it into a zillion pieces.

"What are you doing?" Tamika screams as she holds out her hands in an attempt to catch the falling pieces of paper.

"This is sick. The whole thing is sick," Kylie yells. "And I'm just so sick of everything. Sick of you and Zachary." She looks at me. "And sick of all these games."

"But what about the rest of Beachwood?" Tamika says. "We need the proof. We need to show everyone this list."

"We can tell them." Kylie flings her bag over her shoulder.

"Now, let's go drown our sorrows in mounds of sugar and frosting."

"How can you eat at a time like this?" Abby asks in disbelief. Her hand shoots up to cover her mouth, as if she can't believe she just stood up to crazy Kylie Collins.

Kylie flips around to face Abby. "While the rest of you are surprised, I'm not. These guys are jerks. The paper I just tore doesn't tell us anything new. It only confirms what I've known all along."

Tamika interrupts, "But, Kylie—"

"No buts. You all know I'm right. And anyway, I'm not going to let a bunch of dumb guys get in our way again." She pushes Zoe and Abby out of her path and begins to saunter off. When no one follows, she turns back around. "Come on! I'm dying for some Red Velvet."

Zoe shrugs and glances at the rest of us. "Sounds good to me. My brother can act like a total tool."

We all sheepishly trot behind. *Of all people, Kylie likes sweet Sprinkles? Sweet is not a word I would ever use in the same sentence as Kylie.* And I thought guys texting me was weird.

thirty-seven

"So, how are we going to get the word out about the list?" Tamika asks, while in line outside of Sprinkles.

I hang back a bit, still fuming. *How could I be so stupid?*

"We got the word out about the original three-B through the Internet, so it seems like that's a good way to go. They are calling theirs three-B too, after all," Missy suggests.

Eva twiddles her ear bud. "We should have a little song." She starts warbling, "*Click here to see how the guys are playas. Playas. Playas. Oh yeah. Oh-oh-oh yeah.*"

Zoe and Abby break out in a fit of giggles.

"Seriously, girls. How can we make sure everyone finds out about this?" Tamika asks, tightening up her face.

"Uh, isn't it obvious? Texts, ladies. Texts are the best way to spread something fast," Kylie pipes up.

You should know, I think to myself. It takes all of my strength not to burst out: *Remember someone named Chloe? You ruined her life with one text.* But I've never gotten anywhere in life by being mean. Time to distract myself with the sweet bakery smell.

"Kylie, not that that's not a good idea—it totally is. And you know I love you like a sister . . ." Missy speaks up, steadying herself for the Kylie onslaught, "but do you think texts will *really* get our message out faster than the Internet?"

"Are you kidding me?" Kylie answers, in total shock that her BFF would dare contradict her. "It's instantaneous, total annihilation. People check their accounts at different times, but everyone will see these texts at the exact same second. And bam, we put the boys to bed."

"Kylie's right," Tamika agrees. "If we all text our contacts, we should hit the entire school. Okay, everyone out with their phones!"

Everyone reaches into their bags. I contemplate doing the same, but as much as I want to help other girls avoid feeling the pain I'm currently experiencing, it's not like my contact list is so extensive. In fact, I'm pretty sure that with my teammates texting so furiously, all the numbers I have stored will be covered.

Bzzzzz. Bzzzz. On cue, my phone begins buzzing, as if it's sending me a not-so-gentle reminder. Great, even my phone is in on the conspiracy. I take a deep breath and picture my cupcake. *Caramel cake. Brown sugar frosting. Crunchy nut praline.*

"This place is crazy busy," Jessica says, breaking me from my reverie.

"Yeah, I know. Seriously," Eva agrees, shoving her phone into her baggy pants pocket.

We all take a step closer to the open door. At this point, the smell of cinnamon, sugar, and other delectable goodies is tickling my nose.

I hear someone lick their lips. Tamika. Catching herself mid-lick, a realization washes over her face. "Wait, guys! We never did the last team-building activity!"

Kylie pushes me forward. "Freshmen first."

"Okay, Taylor, you're up." Tamika nods her head in agreement.

Let's just add to my misery. Joy. *What good could Kylie possibly have to say about me?*

"Taylor is athletic," Tamika volunteers.

"Thanks," I say, feeling my cheeks heat up.

"I'll add sweet like a cupcake," Jessica says, smiling at me.

Kylie makes a weird nasal giggle slash snort.

"Thanks, Jess," I answer. "That's very nice of you to say."

"Tall," Eva says.

I'll take tall. "Thank you, Eva."

"Brunette," Missy says.

"Nice," Zoe pipes up.

"Beachwood Basketball Queen," Abby adds.

"Thanks, guys."

"Ugly-duckling-like." Kylie giggles.

My stomach drops.

"What?" Jessica retorts. "Come on, Kylie, that's messed up."

"No, it's not. Taylor's the total ugly-duckling package.

She's coming out of her ugly stage. And one day soon, she'll be a glowing swan."

"Coach said one word, Ky," Tamika reminds Kylie.

"Yeah, but that's one of the best compliments ever," Missy responds.

"Thanks, Miss. Guess you're not a total traitor after all," Kylie continues, having sufficiently embarrassed Missy. "Think about it. She used to be really awkward in middle school and now she's becoming totally gorgeous."

I stare at my sneaks. "Thanks," I squeak. Kylie's right. Coming from her, that's probably the biggest compliment ever. Who knew team building could be sweeter than Sprinkles?

thirty-eight

The next day at fashion show practice, Mrs. Sealer showers Violet with compliment after compliment. I know it's not nice to say this, especially after all my teammates just told me what a good person I am, but if Mrs. Sealer gives Violet another "I hope you remember little ole me when you're famous," I might just throw up in my mouth.

I try to slap a smile on my face, but my patience is seriously depleted—today was just ridiculously insane. After the guys' 3B list got out, more face slaps, foot stomps, and punches to the gut than I've ever seen in my life ensued. And Hannah, of course, proceeded to remind me not once, but four times, why she hangs out at the skate park, and not the beach courts.

Violet turns at the end of the catwalk and strikes a Paris Hilton pose.

Mrs. Sealer claps her hands like a seal. "Bravo! Bravo!"

Ugghhh. I glance at my phone.

DAD: WHERE ARE YOU?????

ME: REHEARSAL?

DAD:	FOR WHAT?
ME:	A FASHION SHOW
DAD:	WHAT????
ME:	4 HANNAH
DAD:	YOU MISSED YOUR TRAINER APPOINTMENT

My stomach sinks. Between fashion show practice, basketball, and the drama over the guys' 3B list, I completely forgot about my Tuesday training appointment. How could I do that? What is wrong with me? Basketball comes first, and I've got to make our game against Richland mean something this time.

ME:	I'LL BE HOME LATER TO WORK OUT IN MY ROOM. THEN, I'LL PRACTICE. SORRY ☹

After Violet's performance, Mrs. Sealer glances down at her clipboard. Her expression changes. "You. Teri." She points at me. "You're next," she says, in an I'm-losing-interest raspy voice.

"Taylor," I say, under my breath. I strap on my red, patent leather heels and begin my strut (the strut I've been practicing whenever my life is not consumed by drama). I stop at the end of the catwalk and pivot. As I'm turning, my heel slips out from under me and I lose my balance. At the last second, I manage to catch myself. *Whoaaa.* Thank god for my basketball balancing skills.

"No. No. No. Wrong. Wrong. Wrong." Mrs. Sealer violently shakes her head.

"Like this." Mrs. Sealer purses her collagen-filled lips and juts her hips as she walks.

I take a few steps backward and try again. As I struggle to strut, I hear some of the other girls break into giggles, and my breathing starts to race. Again.

"No. No. No. More drama. Like Vi."

Impossible. I don't think anyone can be as dramatic as Vi.

I calm my breathing and adjust my heels. Then I take a few steps back, inhale deeply, and sashay down the catwalk. I jut my hips out like I'm trying to knock people over with my hip bones.

"Better. Better," Mrs. Sealer says.

I don't know if she means it or not, but at least the giggles are gone. I glance at her in the hopes of catching sight of a smile, but she's busy staring down at her clipboard.

Finally, Mrs. Sealer looks up. "Missy, you're next," she announces. I allow myself to think: *Maybe she'll smile at me now?* Naturally, that's when she chooses to squash any remaining hope that I actually made real progress. "Show our little Tay Tay how it's done."

Uggh, not that again. "Taylor," I say.

Mrs. Sealer simply shrugs. Then turns her attention to Missy, making it perfectly clear that she's done with me for the day.

I look down at my feet and glumly trudge off the stage. The Ugly Duckling is back with a vengeance.

thirty-nine

"No way!" Hannah yells, limping across her carpet toward her bed. "Who am I going to get to wear designs for a six-foot-tall model?"

I roll my eyes, pulling off the pinned faux-fur vest Hannah's working on.

Hannah falls back on her bed and places her hands in front of her eyes. "Saying you want to quit the fashion show is completely freaking me out. And this is just adding to my horrible day." She sighs.

"Banana, I didn't know you had a bad day! What happened?" I ask.

"I didn't want to upset you. I screwed up my ankle attempting another ollie after school at the skate park." She shows me her bruised ankle.

"Oh my gosh." I don't know what to say. I should have asked Hannah about her limp right away. I'm so selfish. And I don't want Hannah to be in pain AND model-less.

"I know, right? What is it a full moon or something?" She shrugs.

God, I'd be a horrible friend to quit now. "Fine. I'll do it."

I plop in front of Hannah's desk, type in Zach's name, and click on his page. I'm surprised to see that it still says "in a relationship," since I never accepted his request. Not so surprising is the one wall post from Nick that says "3B." *Yeah, three-B all right.*

"I don't get it. Why would Zach try to write that he's in a relationship with me if he was only trying to collect points for some stupid list?" I look over at Hannah who's still sprawled across her bed.

"First off, who cares? Second, I guess guys like Zach know how girls think." Hannah faces me.

"What do you mean?" I ask.

"You need me to tell you?"

I look at her, totally clueless.

"Only that guys who are 'in a relationship' are way hotter than guys who are single," Hannah answers, knowingly.

"Seriously?"

"Yeah, seems that Zach's a very smart guy."

I click on my page and reply to Jessica's post, saying that yes, I will tutor her in math after school tomorrow. Then I robotically fulfill my other duties. "Maybe he was just doing the list thing because he's on the basketball team and feels pressure from his teammates."

"Are you freaking insane?" Hannah shakes her head.

I give Hannah the one answer that I know will make her stop hassling me about my boy problems. "Come on, let's just do my fittings."

"That's what I like to hear!" She gingerly bounces off her bed, keeping weight off her injured right ankle, and grabs her tape measure. "Now, I just need one more measurement so I can put the finishing touches on the top."

I walk over to her so she doesn't have to put pressure on her poor ankle.

She wraps the tape measure across my chest. "You are going to look so fab. Zach will totally regret ever using you as his 'bonus babe.'"

I try to hide my quizzical expression.

Fortunately, Hannah doesn't notice that I'm not buying what she's selling. She's too intent on measuring me . . . *and on sharing her thoughts on the Zach issue.* "Tay, you have to admit that being worth more points is way better than being a regular five-pointer." She playfully punches me in the arm.

"Yeah, it's great."

She pulls the tape measure tighter across my boobs. "Perfect."

I wonder if there is any difference between my chest measurement and my actual boobs. Can it be negative? Am I a scientific marvel?

"Just one more finishing touch." Hannah locks arms with me, and I shoulder her weight as she limps down the hallway toward her design room. When she arrives at the doorway, she grabs a hold of the wall and hobbles into the room.

Meanwhile, I hear Violet's voice downstairs. I peek over the banister and into the open foyer. Matt is standing with her. At first, all I can make out is mumbles. So, not being someone who's willing to pass up on this kind of opportunity, I quietly slip down the steps until I can hear actual words.

"Yup. We're all set," Violet says, handing Matt something in an envelope.

An envelope? Money? I scale a couple more steps. Is Vi running a dating ring? Is she the new B-Dub madam?

"You know I'd do anything for you," Vi adds, wrapping her arm around Matt's shoulders.

They walk away, and I lose sight of them. Then, I hear some lip smacking coming from the great room.

My curiosity quickly wins out. I tiptoe down the rest of the steps and peek in. Unfortunately, from my vantage point, I can't spot the happy couple. Time to take another step. I close my eyes and count to three. *One, two, three.* . . . Opening them, I hold my breath and see . . .

Vi sprawled out across the coach, licking a lollipop. Matt is gone.

"Hey, Taylor!" Hannah's mom, Celia, steps next to me, her matching Montgomery-platinum hair bouncing as she walks.

I try to come up with a spur-of-the-moment lie. "Uh . . . I was . . . uh . . ." Lying has never been my thing. "Thinking about getting something to eat, but then I changed my mind."

"How's basketball?" She smiles, oblivious to my sleuthing. "Sorry to hear about Richland. Can you believe you're going to face them again on Saturday?"

My stomach flips for a zillion different reasons. Why was I spying on Vi and Matt? And how am I going to prepare for the biggest game of my life on Saturday?

After I'm done chatting basketball with Celia, I climb the steps two at a time (spider long–legs are good for something) and join Hannah in her bedroom.

"While I'm stuck in here, why don't you raid my closet for an outfit for tomorrow?" Hannah says, moving the mountains of ripped magazines surrounding her on her bed.

Ignoring her, I grab the remote and flick the TV on. My head is spinning.

Hannah's sprawled on her bed again, this time with her foot resting on a pillow. "Come on. Grab my Rebecca and Wolf ebony blazer and a black pair of heels."

"I'm a size ten," I remind her.

"Well, okay, Tay, I'll give you that. But you need practice. Like basketball. You need to wear the heels the rest of the week so you won't be so nervous on the runway."

I stare at her like she has ten heads. Why do people keep thinking that shoe sizes are irrelevant?

"How about the heels you wore today during the rehearsal?" Hannah pulls the caramel threaded needle through the fur.

I move toward the door to grab the red heels from my bag. "These?"

Hannah scrunches her nose at my scarlet pumps. "Never mind." She rests the fur vest on her lap. "Grab my black blazer and pair it with skinny jeans and a cool, loud tee. Then, see if your mom can take you out to snag a pair of black heels or something. Save the red ones for the show."

I smile and tug the blazer off the hanger. "It's too small."

"Shrunken blazers are hip right now. Trust me." Hannah grabs a magazine off her bed, shuffles through a few pages, and holds it up to me. "See. Now find a tee like this one." She points at the skinny-mini model.

I peruse the closet for a T-shirt big enough to fit me. "How about this one?" I peek out, holding a lavender Billabong V-neck with white embellished flowers across the front.

"Perfect." Hannah grins, satisfied.

Then I eye Hannah's denim selection. It's one thing to squeeze into one of her tees, but forget about her size-two jeans. Time to cut my losses. "And I have the perfect pair of jeans at home." I say, mustering up enthusiasm I didn't know I had.

"Sweet," Hannah says, a grin the size of Beachwood's football field on her face. "Don't you just love the creative process?"

"Yeah. Love it." I pump my fist.

Although fashion is Hannah's thing, I'll admit it—it's kind of growing on me. Especially ever since I began walking the runway. I'm actually getting the hang of this outfit thing, loving all the attention (even if it was only for the 3B list), and think I'm starting to feel . . . well, *pretty*.

forty

I hightail it home from Hannah's when I realize it's past nine and I haven't touched my homework. After I rush through my back door, I scale the steps.

"Spider!" My dad flips the television off and stands up. His face is red. "First, you skip your trainer appointment, then you show up at home past nine when you still have to work out?"

"Sorry. I lost track of time." I stop at the bottom step. "I'll go work out now in my room." I jump the steps two at a time.

"Zach called me today," Dad announces.

"What?" I snap my head back to face him.

"Are you parking with him in the hills?"

Did my dad seriously just ask me that? "No. What did *he* want?"

He raises his right eyebrow. "Zach wants to practice with me. He wants me to train him."

"Seriously?"

My dad's twisted face relaxes a bit. "So, he'll be coming around a few times a week."

Yikes.

"Anyway, remember to do your shoulder, quad, and calf work since you missed training today. The last thing you need is an injury."

I muster up a grin, even though I'm exhausted. "Thanks, Dad," I say and barrel up the rest of the steps.

Before I turn into my room, I cross the hallway to the master suite and peek in on Mom. Empty. I guess she's out on one of her so-called auditions. Why is she never around lately? I could really use some motherly advice right about now.

Once I'm in my room, I grab a Nerf ball from my desk.

"Collins passes the ball to Thomas. She sets up for the three . . ." I take a step backward and take a shot. "And the crowd erupts! I've never heard them cheer this loud before for a state championship game. Amazing!"

I pick the ball up off the floor, back up, and run toward the net, dunking over and over again until I'm exhausted. "Watch Thomas dunk," I announce in my commentator voice, and giggle at the made-up WNBA commentary. One day I'll dunk for real.

After I finish a quick workout, my homework beckons, so I begrudgingly crack open *Catcher in the Rye* and log onto my computer. I should tackle my critical essay, but before I do, I quickly type a "happy birthday" to Zoe, chat with Tamika, and check my messages. In between, I make a short list:

Reasons Why Zach Did the 3B List

1. If he didn't do it, the guys would kick him off the team.
2. The team threatened to beat up his little sister.
3. His mom is sick and the prize for winning is something she's always wanted.
4. He really is a jerk ☹

And then I pass out before ever touching my paper.

forty-one

The next day Hannah taps me with one of her crutches as I adjust my blazer. (She calls it "shrunken." I call it "teeny tiny.") Speaking of Hannah, I took her advice and paired the blazer with the loudest shirt I could think of—an oversized bright orange T-shirt from basketball camp. (Her Billabong tee ended up being too short by three inches). Then I threw on stonewashed blue skinny jeans from my mom's *L.A. High* days and my red pumps. I figure it's best to practice in the shoes I'm actually going to be wearing. In my pre–fashion show days, I wouldn't have had the guts to wear something like this, but at this point, who cares? I survived life as a bonus babe and dogged my SoCal tryout. I might as well tackle the fashion scene. What else do I have to lose?

Looking at Hannah with her crutches, I realize that there are more important things to be worrying about than my new ensemble. "So, Banana, what did the doc say?" I ask.

Hannah leans on her crutches. "It's a third-degree sprain. No skateboarding for six weeks."

I let out a deep breath and fall into best-friend mode.

Bending down to hug her, I stumble a bit on the heels and have to catch myself on my locker. "What about the fashion show?"

"The doc said I can still do it. But, it's going to totally stink." She blankly stares. "I feel like I'm never going to be able to pull it off. I have so much to do."

"I'll help you." I smile and shut my locker.

Hannah takes another look at me. "What the heck are you wearing?"

"Like it?" I spin around the way Mrs. Sealer taught us and stumble some more on my heels.

"It's, uh, different," Hannah says, blinking her eyes a few times.

"I knew you'd be impressed." I even open up my blazer and jut my hips out Violet-style. "I took your advice after all."

"Okay, as your best friend it's my duty to tell you . . . Taylor, your outfit is . . . shall we say, not working?"

"What? I did what we talked about." I say, defensively.

"Yeah . . . you did. But maybe you took things a little too literally. If you're going to wear a camp T-shirt, then stick with a smaller version and pair it with your usual sweats and sneaks. And if you're going for the blazer, skinny jeans, and heels look, then you need a more form fitting, longer tee underneath. Or else, just go back to the way you used to dress. At least it's consistent."

"But, you told me to wear a loud T-shirt." I look down at my orange shirt.

"A loud, small one, like the one I gave you or something cute. And red pumps don't match jail-cell orange." She juts out her lower lip. "Sorry."

I force a smile and swallow a lump in my throat, not wanting Hannah to see that ever since the 3B list, I'm feeling pretty low. I mean, she has enough stuff to deal with right now without her BMF (Best Model Friend) getting all emotional. "I'll just change in the locker room."

"Do you have an extra pair of sweats in your locker?" She sighs.

"I'm good." *This whole fashion thing is way too much hassle. Jeans and T-shirts from now on.*

Hannah whimpers, resting her crutches next to my locker. "How am I going to walk the runway with you at the end of the show?"

"You can trick out your cast and your crutches and be the most stylish gimp out there."

She smiles and lifts her crutch in the air, staring at it. "You're right. Screw my ankle." Hannah snatches back the Volcom tote.

I give Hannah one last hug before the bell rings. Then, I head toward English class and Matt who is probably enjoying a post-Vi afterglow. Yuck.

forty-two

I make a right into the classroom and settle into my seat. Fortunately, Mr. Ludwig is scribbling on the board, so he doesn't notice that I'm a minute late. I open up to a blank page in my notebook and frantically write my Word of the Day. Since I fell asleep without touching my homework, I've spent the whole day trying to catch up. Plus, I can't stop thinking about my mom. When I went into her room this morning, she was still sleeping, and normally, she never misses an opportunity to send me off to school.

All of a sudden, I feel the point of something hard digging into my back. I reach around to grab for it, and am excited to discover that the offending object is Matt's leather bound notebook.

"What's this, party boy?" I turn around and pry the notebook from his grasp.

"Easy there. You better simmer down now or I won't show you what I wrote last night." Matt's M&M eyes are the size of saucers.

"That'd be difficult seeing as I'm already holding a certain something in my hands." I wave the notebook at him.

"Oh, you think you're so fast, Miss Center?"

"You know it!" I smile at him and open up the notebook.

Red

Lips.

Cheeks on a cold winter day.

Hearts.

Tell me, Sunshine, what should I say?

When I'm finished, I stare at the poem for a few more seconds, wondering if sex really does make a guy into mush. At least that's what Hannah always says. She says girls have power over some guys. By the looks of this poem, I think she's right. I mean, Vi certainly has a strong hold on Matt. She's turning him into a complete mess, especially when she wears red silk tanks, like she did yesterday.

"Are you two sharing your Word of the Day?" Mr. Ludwig stops at our desks. Matt quickly shuts his notebook.

"Ummm. Yup, Mr. Ludwig. We bring in extra assignments to go with our Word of the Day theme." Matt grins, showing off his chipped incisor.

"I see." Ludwig lifts his round glasses for a second and eases into a smile. "It's nice to see you both going the extra mile." He puffs his chest out a bit and moves on to his next victim.

We both smirk and I hand him back his book.

"Anyway, about your poem . . ." I begin, tentatively. "Are you and Vi . . ."

That's when I'm rudely interrupted. "Hey, Matthew," Allison Webb yells from across the room after Mr. Ludwig steps into the hallway to speak with the assistant principal. "We had fun last night."

Matt gives Allison a small grin.

"Are you hooking up with Violet?" I blurt out.

Matt cracks his knuckles. "Uh . . . I don't know if you would exactly call it hooking up. We've hung out a few times."

I cross my arms in front of my chest.

"Hey, Teri!" Allison motions at me with one hand and runs her fingers through her ebony hair with the other. "Teri," she says again.

"Taylor," I say and smile at Allison. I can manage to be nice even if she can't.

"Whatever. Nice outfit." She flips open her cell phone and tilts her head, pushing the keys. "You know, the inmate-picking-up-trash look suits you."

Fourteen pairs of eyes descend on me. I cross my arms in front of my orange T-shirt and blazer. I so should have changed even if it meant I had to take the late hit from Ludwig.

"Thank you." I attempt to pay it forward. I swallow and smooth my jeans down. Then, I stare at the clock. But, the minute hand is moving even slower now than it does during one of Mr. Ludwig's lectures.

"Duh . . . I was just kidding," she enunciates. She rolls her heavily massacred eyes.

Oh, no, she didn't. I feel a *kaboom* in my chest as if someone punched me. *Am I dying?* I search for the white light.

"Taylor." Matt shakes my arm a bit.

Okay, I guess I didn't die.

I stand up gingerly and slink toward the hallway and Mr. Ludwig.

Then, I stop and take a deep breath. "Annie," I say, digging deep for my inner beast like I do when I'm driving toward the basket.

She stops texting and glares at me.

"I mean, *Allison.* My bad." I fake giggle. "I was, uh, seeing how long it would take for someone to bust me for what I was wearing this morning. It's an experiment for psychology to see who the most materialistic girls at school are. You know, the ones who take being shallow to a whole new level."

Allison opens her mouth, as if to shut me down again, but then . . . nothing. Her lips tighten and she returns to her phone.

I let out a deep breath, feeling spent. *I left a Violet-girl speechless.* My classmates turn back to their Word of the Day and, I swear, a few actually chuckle and grin at me.

Then, the bell rings.

"Hey." Matt pokes me with his index finger. "Nice one."

I toss my bag over my shoulder and stand up, debating

whether I should be like *yeah, you know it* or *nah, it was rude of me.*

But, a Violet-girl doesn't give up that easily. Allison steps in front of me. "Didn't mean to make you so upset," she says.

I try to rally myself for my second comeback of the day, but my mind is blank.

"You should be happy. I mean, *I* cared enough to ask about *your* outfit." She looks me up and down.

"Back off, Ally," Matt says, rolling his eyes. "You're just pissed Taylor made you look bad." He grabs my hand and pulls me into the hallway. Once we're out of the classroom, he looks into my eyes as if he and I are the only two people on the planet. This is pretty hard to pull off considering that this is happening during insanely busy in-between-classes time.

Zach steps in front of Matt.

"How's my girl?"

I look into Zach's big, brown eyes, think back to my made-up list of reasons for why Zach would participate in the 3B list, and cross my fingers. "Did the team threaten to beat up your sister?"

"Huh?"

"Never mind." I turn around and leave Zach standing there. Alone.

forty-three

I push the Beachwood doors open after school and the bright February sun immediately warms my face. After a few cloudy, rainy days, the sun feels energizing. If I walk fast, I'll make it home just in time to fit in everything. I worked out a plan during eighth period. Jessica and I are going to Skype tutor. Then, afterward, my dad and I can play Horse from four to four-thirty. After that, practice at five and Hannah's at seven for more fittings. Then, back at my house by eight thirty to hopefully chat with Mom and find out what the heck is going on before she hits the sack. And finally, homework.

"No practice?" Matt asks, catching up with me.

"It's late today." I look around. "Where's your number-one girl, Vi?"

"Wait, what—" Matt begins.

Before he can finish his thought, I feel a yank on my arm. Hannah. "Thank god you're not at practice. I need you for some last minute alterations." When I turn around to face her, her rosy cheeks are way blotchy. Blotchy cheeks on Hannah mean she's mega stressed. "My house NOW." She points at me with her crutch. Then, she glances at Matt and switches her voice to sweet. "Hey, Matt."

"Hey." Matt grins and his deep dimples pop.

"Sorry, Banana. But I have to help out Jessica and I have practice at five. I'll come right over after prac—"

"This is important!" She slams her tricked out crutch on the floor. "Plus, Missy said that you said you aren't walking the runway for me on Friday night after all."

"Yes, I am." My face twists.

"I'm totally one hundred percent counting on you." She waves her crutch in the air.

"And who are you going to believe. Me or Missy?" I answer, my hands on my hips.

"Okay, you got me there. Just don't let me down." She crutches away, violently swinging her legs.

Urgh. I stomp toward the door. When I feel Matt following me, I stop and turn around. "Look, no offense," I say. "But, I'm busy. So, if you have a bus or a Violet to catch, you should probably just go ahead and do that."

Matt just stands there. And that's when I realize the enormity of what I just said. *What has gotten into me?* Two mean moments in one day. I never act like this. "I'm sorry," I quickly add. "I didn't mean that . . . I guess I'm just stressed."

"I'm going the same way you are." He's totally not fazed.

"Oh, okay. You should have just said that," I reply, and resume my walk.

For a few blocks, we walk together in silence. Me: Patrick. Him: SpongeBob. Me: Yogi Bear. Him: Boo Boo. Me: Big Bird. Him: Elmo. Or to make a long story short. Me: Alone for the rest of my life because Zach three-B'ed me. Him: With Vi. Us: Just friends with a massive height difference.

Once we clear the sea grass and reach the beach, I leave the wooden path, shed my sneaks and sink my sore toes into the smooth sand. Then I pull out my phone to check the time. Don't want to mess up my schedule for the night.

"You know, Taylor, it's really nice what you're doing for Hannah," Matt says, perking up out of the blue.

I run my toes over the tiny, multicolored pebbles that line the shore.

"What do you mean?" As I glimpse at his tiny feet one more time to see if they grew since last week, I notice how worn out his Nikes look.

"Putting yourself out there for your friend." He pauses. "But be careful."

He plops down on the sand, balancing his arms on his knees in his cute compact kind of way. I follow and fall down next to him dangling my legs out across the sand, as long and lanky as ever. I check my phone again. I have twenty minutes until I have to help Jessica out.

"But, sometimes there's a too-nice line. Today during English was the first time I've ever seen you put someone in their place."

I lean back and sink my fingers into the cool sand.

"I get it. Wanting to make everyone happy. I do it too sometimes," Matt says.

"When did you get all psychoanalyst? I thought your expertise was girls."

"Seriously. I just get it, that's it. Especially ever since . . ."

I wait for Matt to tell me, but he stops. So, I spill instead. "Me too. I've been trying to make people happy since . . . well, since birth. Ever since my dad gave up on his dreams of the NBA because I was born." A white crest smashes into a cliff.

Matt turns his head toward mine.

I don't know why I'm spilling everything, but once I start I can't stop. "I feel horrible about it. And now I have the chance to be amazing at basketball and make it to the WNBA and make him really proud of me, so he never regrets what he did. Even though I know he does. Regret it. I mean. And I don't know if I'll ever make that right."

Matt lets out a deep breath and nods. "Do you even like basketball?"

"I love basketball," I say, without hesitation. What does he mean by *that*? I've known plenty of girls that played for the wrong reasons, eventually quitting. But basketball is my life. I can't imagine surviving without it.

Matt tilts his head and looks at me out of the corner of his eye. A breeze rustles my ponytail and a shiver runs up my back. Not a cold shiver, but a comfy shiver.

"I've always loved basketball. I'm the happiest when I'm out on the court," I explain.

"But you're happy at other times too, right? Like, right now?" He grins impishly. Then he pulls up his sleeve and rests his arms on his knees, revealing the scar that I noticed earlier.

I stare at the mark and wonder at the story behind it. "What's this?"

"A scar."

"Obviously, genius." I roll my eyes. "But, from what?"

He continues to stare at the crashing waves and lets out a deep breath. "I'm sure you heard all the stuff about me being broke and all. Well, it's true. All of it." He shifts in the sand. "A little less than a year ago, me and my dad were going to Whole Foods to pick up some groceries." He lets out another breath. "At some point on our way, there was this huge slam. When I came to, I was in the hospital and my arm was all bruised up. But, besides that and a few cuts on my left leg, I was okay. My dad, however, wasn't. He took the bulk of the impact because the car plowed us on the driver's side."

I reach out to touch his arm. "Oh, god. What was wrong with him?"

Matt flinches at first at my touch, but then composes himself. "He was . . . uh," he looks me directly in the eyes. "He was paralyzed and in a coma."

"I'm so sorry." I begin rubbing his arm.

Now, he shivers. "Yeah, me too. But, honestly, my dad's lucky to be alive."

"How is he now?" I picture the scene and can't help but imagine how I'd feel if it were my mom or dad.

"He's beating the odds. I knew he would." He grins.

"He sounds like a tough cookie."

"Oh, definitely. That's my dad." His grin grows larger for a second, but then he shakes his head. "But he's on oxygen twenty-four-seven and we're constantly at the emergency room because we can almost never get his breathing stabilized at home."

"Oh, god."

"Yeah, docs say they don't know how much more time he has."

"I'm so incredibly sorry," I say again, wondering what it must be like to have to take care of your own parent.

"You kind of get used to it." He rubs his eyes. "But, my life used to be a lot easier before the accident. After the medical bills piled up because my dad lost his job, we moved from our house in Beverly Hills to a tiny, decrepit apartment outside L.A. I came to Beachwood because they gave me a free ride for lacrosse. So I'm officially a charity case."

My stomach sinks. "No, you're not. I can't imagine what you're going through." I stare at his school-store-bought sweatshirt. I guess clothes aren't really at the top of the list when you're worried about food and stuff.

"Enough about me and my depressing life." He straightens up. "All I'm saying is it's good to be nice to everyone, but sometimes you have to be nice to yourself too."

I mull this one over and over. I mean, I *do* do a lot for everyone . . . Then I jump up and blurt out, "Enough upsetting stuff." I put my hand out and help Matt up.

The second he's on his feet, I realize that I'm still holding his hand and abruptly take mine back. Totally embarrassed, I quickly begin shuffling down the beach. Despite our height disparity, Matt matches me, stride for stride. And sometimes, I swear, I think I feel him reaching for my hand. But, I could be completely imagining it. Or worse, Matt just wants to add me to his growing 3B list.

Can't believe his name was on the list too. How could someone who seems so sweet be so full of it? Plus, if he's trying to hold my hand again, what is he hoping for? More points? *Are there any nice guys left on this planet?*

As we approach my house, I try to think of what I'm supposed to say in a situation like this, but Matt beats me to the punch. "I'm so sorry, Taylor. I gotta go. I'm late for the bus and my dad needs me." And with that, Matt Moore sprints down my street.

Good-bye, Matt the Mysterious. Hello, my Great Aunt Sally future.

forty-four

"Finally." My dad's face lights up as I walk through the back door. He points the remote at the flat screen.

For once in my life, I ignore the screen flashing to black and head toward the winding staircase.

"We need to talk," he blurts out.

I freeze, and then retreat back down the beige steps. My heart races. He's finally going to drop the bomb about what's going on with Mom.

"What's up?" My heart is beating so hard I can hear it.

He crosses his arms in front of his worn out and ripped blue Beachwood Academy tee. "Did you settle everything with Kylie?"

Kylie? *Wait, what?* The whole Kylie thing seems as if it happened a million years ago. I jolt my memory. "Yeah," I say.

His eyebrows almost touch his hairline. "And . . ."

I glance at the microwave to check the time.

"Eek! Dad, I have to help Jessica with her math." I charge up the steps.

"Wait, Taylor. Saturday's game is huge." He chases after

me. "Why don't you meet me outside and shoot some free throws? You *did* miss five out of nine attempts the other night. Then we can play some one-on-one and work on your fade away before Richland on Saturday."

"I'll be out in fifteen minutes," I shout as I reach my room. I quickly change into my practice clothes and boot up my computer.

I let out a deep breath, swallow the lump in my throat, and face a pixilated Jessica, who's waving and smiling at me through Skype.

"Hey, Tay. You ready to tutor me?"

After another deep breath, a few flushes creep up my back and I say, "Yup."

So much for Matt's advice. Taylor the People Pleaser strikes again.

forty-five

Jessica's Skype tutoring session ends up lasting way longer than I expected. So long, in fact, that I have to cut out my computer duties entirely, or else skip hoops time with Dad. Naturally, given all my recent basketball mishaps, I choose practicing with my father over commenting on people's posts. But even then, I only make eight free throws before I have to sprint to practice.

I arrive at practice a couple minutes late to the sound of Coach Jackson saying, "Okay, girls. Grab one of the jump ropes Coach Martie laid out on the court. Richland ran circles around us the last time, and believe me, that won't happen again."

The team groans and one by one we pick up our jump ropes. As I'm uncoiling a blue one, I decide I like Martie's team building much better. Still, I quickly find a spot in the rear corner, as far away from everyone as possible. Despite my lack of interest in jumping rope, it's officially time to get into my zone.

Coach Jackson blows the whistle and twenty plastic

covered jump ropes smack the ground like ticking clocks. At first, I embrace the sweating and the heat build-up. I mean, there's always that point in practice where you want to quit but you force yourself to cross your limit and boom, you feel euphoric. Except this time my breath leaves my lungs like I'm sucking on a vacuum. *What, the???*

Coach immediately notices that I've stopped jumping. "Taylor, are you up for this?"

"Yeah," I say as I grab the handles and begin again. Coach is right that we can't let Richland cream us another time. Maybe my plan isn't so well-advised though, because once again, I begin to sweat and feel my heart speed up. I stop mid-jump.

"Come on, Taylor," Tamika says, wiping the sweat from her face with the back of her hand.

I start up again and catch sight of Kylie looking at me out of the corner of her eye.

"You look really pale, Taylor," Eva gasps between breaths, staring at me as the jump rope swings around and around.

The pasty comment. That's it. I must be having a heart attack. Thank you, Internet research for saving my life. A lightening bolt rips through my stomach.

I stop for good, drop the rope, and walk toward the hallway. I think to myself: *All I need is a drink. Just one drink. After that, I'll be fine.* And honestly, what else am I supposed to think? I have no choice. I have to get back on the court. Our big game is Saturday.

On my way to the hallway water fountain, I almost topple into the boys' basketball team as they're coming in from their beach run.

As I bend down to sip the water, I feel a gentle graze against my hip. When I look up, Zach's amber eye-sprinkles meet mine. He smiles.

I choke on the water.

"Taylor, are you choking?" The boys' basketball coach approaches me. I feel my face flush, and I gasp as I attempt to catch my breath. My cheeks burn like I stuck my head in an oven.

"I'm fine," I squeak and lower my face into the water fountain again. But, it's not working.

"Do you need the trainer?" The basketball coach leans so far into the water fountain that he's almost nose to nose with me. So close, in fact, that I can smell his Old Spice.

"No." Gasp. "Really." Gasp. "I'm." Gasp. "Fine."

"Are you sure?" He tilts his head like a concerned parent. I nod.

He abruptly turns around. "Show's over, boys. Into the weight room!" The entire boys' basketball team files by, some snickering, some staring. Most are clearly disappointed that the girls' center is not going to need mouth-to-mouth resuscitation from their ancient coach.

Zach lingers. "You feeling okay?" he asks.

"Yeah." I avoid his eyes and dip my head in for some more water.

"Are you still upset about that stupid list? The whole thing was bogus."

A shiver (the kind that only Zach can cause) runs up my spine. When I look up, he's smiling.

"Come on, lover boy," the boys' coach yells.

I dip my head back into the water fountain. And this time when I look up, Zach's gone.

forty-six

When I finally return to practice, I quickly grab my jump rope from the hardwood floor in an attempt to make up for lost time. As I'm about to resume jumping, Coach Martie comes over to me. "Why don't you take a break, Thomas?"

I nod, find a spot on the bleachers, and pop a cross-legged squat on the sidelines. At first, I attempt to be a good sport and cheer for my teammates. But it only takes ten seconds of sitting there on the sidelines, watching my teammates playing, for me to fall apart. *How did I get here?* I think. This is my favorite season. This is basketball. And basketball is in my blood.

Fortunately, Coach Jackson comes to my rescue. "Taylor," she calls over. "Press break drill."

I jog out toward my spot on the foul line, ready to practice breaking the full-court opposing team's defense. Richland always has a nasty press. In fact, during our game on Friday, they snagged four steals in the first quarter from their press.

Kylie inbounds the ball to Tamika who chest passes to Eva. I wait for Tamika's pick. Then, I sprint toward her.

Coach Jackson tweets her whistle. "No. No. No, Taylor. Come on. Pay attention!" she shouts.

Martie gives me a quasi-comforting smile. But in light of all that's happened, I'm not entirely sure if she's trying to make me feel better or if she just pities me.

I know I wasn't supposed to run toward Tamika, but I can't remember this play. A play I've practiced and executed hundreds of times. And since Coach Jackson is giving me the kind of stare that Kylie gives the people who cross her before she's about to incinerate them with her eyes, I don't dare to ask what I missed.

"Let's try it again." Coach lets out a deep breath.

Unfortunately, things do not improve from there. In fact, we (and by we, I mean *I*) mess up the play four more times. Coach Jackson is so annoyed that she has us run four suicides (one per mess up), as she and Martie duck away for a water break of their own.

"Thanks, Taylor," Kylie says to me, her arms crossed in front of her chest.

"Yeah." Eva glares at me, tapping her finger on the side of a plastic water bottle.

"What's going on with you, Tay?" Tamika says, pityingly. "You're completely out of it."

"Nothing." I look down at the black line painted across the tan hardwood floor.

"Are your parents getting a divorce?" Missy asks, gliding the lip-gloss wand across her bottom lip.

"What would make you think that?" I ask, wondering for a second if maybe that's why my mom has been M.I.A. so much.

The girls gather around me for an impromptu team meeting. Kylie looks up from placing her ball on the metal rack.

"Or are you in that really weird part of therapy when you realize everything in your world is a nightmare and you're super messed up? I swear, it gets better after that," Missy adds, twisting the cap back on the tube.

"No therapy. I'm fine."

"You don't go to therapy?" Missy looks at me like I announced that I haven't taken a bath in three weeks. "Everyone goes to therapy."

I continue to stare at the floor and feel my heart pound.

"No, seriously, tell me. Are you in therapy about the Zach thing?" Missy's blue eyes bug.

"That's messed up," Kylie says, smacking Missy's side.

Tamika rolls her eyes and lets out a loud sigh. "I'm so tired of hearing about guys, especially Zachary Murphy. We have a huge game on Saturday, one that could cost us our playoff bid. What are the guys doing days before a game? Not worrying about us."

And that's when I find my voice. "Honestly, Tamika, when are they ever?"

forty-seven

When I finally arrive home after texting Hannah I'm too tired to make it (she was not happy), I scale the steps, eager to check on my mom. I gingerly open my parents' bedroom door and peek inside. My mom's lying on her bed. The glow of the television lights her face.

"Hey," I say to her, taking a seat on the edge of her king-sized mattress.

"How are you?" My mom raises a cracker to her mouth, then makes a face and decides against it.

"Good, Mom. But, more importantly, how are you? What's going on?"

She holds up her hand. "Don't worry about me. I'm fine."

"You don't look fine. Are you sick or something?"

"I'm just busy. That's all." Her cell phone buzzes on her nightstand. She picks it up and motions for me to leave.

"Whatever," I swallow a lump in my throat and walk back toward my bedroom.

But when I swing open my bedroom door, my dreams of a good pillow pounding are dashed. Turns out, someone else is already occupying the pillow area.

"Hey," Zach says, from his perch on my bed.

I shut my door, take a deep breath, and open it again. Sure enough, Zachary Murphy is still there. "What are you doing here?" I ask. Zach is lying on my bed. Watching television. In my bedroom. And I'm not even dreaming.

"Waiting for you, Spider." He smiles, showing off his single dimple. "Since you're blowing me off, I figured I'd wait for you in your bedroom before I train with your dad."

He sits up and pats a spot next to him on the mattress.

Zach wants me to sit on my bed with him.

"I'm not blowing you off," I say, keeping my eyes downcast so I don't have to look at him. My fear is that if I look him in the eye, I won't be able to keep the anger flowing. It's hard to stay mad at someone who makes me tingle all over.

"Yes, you are."

"No, seriously, I'm not." I would hate for Zach to think that. I would never blow off anyone. I'm the girl who always includes everyone. "It's just the list . . ." I start to explain as I take a seat at my desk chair, which I promptly roll as far away from Zach as possible.

Zach gazes at me. "I know I screwed up with the list and everything. But I was just going along with the guys. I can't get you out of my head."

Peer pressure. I knew it.

"No other girl gets what it takes to be an elite athlete." He stands up and walks toward me, squatting in front of me so we're nose to nose. "Nobody else gets it. Gets me like you do."

I stare at my pastel blue carpet. Zach is really the *only* guy at Beachwood perfect for me. And he pretty much just told me that he thinks I'm perfect for him. Maybe my friends would understand after all. You know, if I kiss him one more time.

Then Zach does something that would seem to make my decision for me. He grabs my hand.

I stand up.

We're still nose-to-nose.

I take a step backward.

Zach takes a step toward me.

We step like this for a few more minutes until we resemble a couple from *Dancing with the Stars*. I shimmy toward my door. He follows my lead.

"I'm really sorry, but I have a ton of homework," I say. I can't let Zachary Murphy distract me further from school. I've already used up all my excuses, especially in English.

Zach bends down and nuzzles my neck, pressing me against the door. "I can tutor you . . ." he whispers.

My knees buckle and tiny electric shocks run up my back. *How can someone acting so bad smell so yummy?*

"Really, Zach. I'm sorry. . . ."

"You're making me crazy," he whispers again and his hot breath tickles my neck.

More tingles and flushes. Good flushes. Amazing flushes.

Flushes that make me want to roll around with Zach for the night.

He pulls away from me and grabs my Nerf ball, setting up for a shot. "Here's the deal. If I make it, I get to hang out here with you as long as I want to. If I miss, I'll leave."

He spins and takes a fade away shot. The ball hits the rim and bounces away from my closet.

Zach shrugs his shoulders. Without saying another word, he gently kisses my cheek and walks out the door.

I let out a deep breath and fall face first on my bed. Now I officially don't know what to think.

forty-eight

I sleep through my alarm the next morning and barely make it to school on time. I hightail it to my locker, and as I swing it open, a purple envelope falls out, hitting my Nike flip-flops. *What the?*

Before I can open up the envelope, Hannah appears. "I'm only forgiving you for ditching me yesterday because you're my BMF," she says, shuffling around on her crutches. "Plus, I don't think I can handle another letdown."

"I'm so sorry, Banana." I look down at my black-and-blue "3B 4 a 3Peat" tank, warm-up jacket, sweats, and sneaks, and can't help but smile. A Taylor Thomas outfit. I was way too tired this morning to coordinate another sexy, scarlet outfit. But, I did manage some red lip gloss. "Do you need me to carry your stuff around again today?" I ask her.

"Nah, that's okay. I'm 'strong like bull.'" She does a mock-Arnold bicep curl and leans to the side to show me her Element bag covered in micro toy skateboards. Then, she notices the card. "What's that?" she asks, pointing to it with her newly tricked-out-with-multicolored-sharpie designed crutch.

"It was in my locker," I answer. Glancing at the purple

envelope, I see that my name is written out on the front in black marker.

Hannah squeals. "You gotta let me see it!" She hobbles behind me into my homeroom. I take a seat at my desk, and she leans over as I carefully peel the envelope open and pull out the white card inside. On the front is a simple red heart sketched using a crayon. Inside, scrawled in black ink, it says, "Taylor. Meet me at the beach courts at 8 p.m. on Friday night."

"Oh my god!!!!!" She yanks on my arm, teetering on her crutches. "What are you going to do? Are you going to go?"

I scan the card. No signature. I shove it inside my notebook. A year ago, even a week ago, I would be totally blissful. But not today. Today it makes me feel flushed, hot, and weird. And besides which, I have a basketball game to think about.

"Taylor! You have to go!" Hannah urges, interrupting my thoughts.

I'm so on edge that I almost jump out of my seat at the sound of her voice. "Uh, no. I don't know. . . ."

"Uggh. You're unbelievable," she says before hobbling out of the room.

As soon as she's out the door, I sneak a peek at Matt from my seat who's chatting with Abby outside the door, feeling awkward about spilling my life story to him yesterday on the beach.

Matt catches me looking at him and grins, showing off his dimples. *I'm such a sucker for dimples.*

He walks over to me, squats down, and lowers his voice, "Do you have any plans on Saturday night?"

"Huh?" I ask, leaning on my notebook.

"There's this poetry slam thing going on at a coffee shop that I wanted to check out. Do you want to go?"

"Uh . . . I, uh."

"Never mind." He takes off toward the doorway even though homeroom isn't yet over.

"No. Wait, Matt—" I flip around in my chair, causing my notebook to fall off my desk. Out tumbles the card. I grab both, and when I look up, Matt's gone.

Before I can jog out the door to look for him, Abby stops me. "Taylor, did you do your bio homework?" she asks.

Bio happens to be the one class I actually did my homework for. (Granted, I did it while Jessica was independently practicing math problems during our Skype tutoring session.) And I can't leave a teammate hanging. "Yeah. I grab my purple Five Star one-subject notebook. "Everything is right here." I open up to the page and hand the notebook over to her. "Let me know if you have any questions." I smile.

"Thanks," she says.

Then, I sprint out the door. But instead of finding Matt calmly walking down the hallway, I catch him holding Nick against the lockers by his throat. *What the?!?*

"Say you're sorry," I hear Matt shout. He punches Nick in the face with his free hand. A group gathers around the fight.

Nick is visibly shaking.

"Say you're sorry!" Bam! Matt slams Nick against the locker.

I push through the growing crowd.

"Sorry!" Nick squeals. Matt lets go and Nick falls down to the ground.

As Nick unsteadily pushes himself up, giving Matt a look that says, "Dude, you're crazy," a security guard grabs Matt. He then hustles them both through the crowd toward the administration office.

Hannah crutches up next to me and squeezes my hand. "That was crazy. I got here a couple minutes before you did."

"What happened?" I ask. "I was just talking to Matt in homeroom."

"I've never seen him like this. Nick was messing around, calling Patrick 'stump man,' and kicking his wheelchair. Matt saw what was going on and freaked out. Then, he grabbed Nick and shoved him up against the locker until he apologized. It was crazy," Hannah recounts. "What did you say to him to make him flip out?"

"Me? Uh . . . nothing," I insist. "It's just that Matt . . ." I stop myself. Even though I know the real reason Matt lost it, I can't spill his secret.

Sweet Matt Moore brought to blows. What is going on?

forty-nine

Matt's seat is empty during English class. As I hear notebooks rustling open to the Word of the Day, I wonder: *Did he get suspended?* Or worse, did he get kicked out of Beachwood for good? What will he do?

"Taylor, can you please bring up your notebook, so I can check your Word-of-the-Day progress?" Mr. Ludwig asks from behind his cherry wood desk.

Eeek. I've been so busy helping out Hannah, practicing with my dad, tutoring Jessica, and prepping for Saturday's basketball game that I haven't done my homework since last week. I open up my notebook and slowly walk up to Ludwig's desk.

He looks down at the blank pages. "There's nothing here except silly lists."

Allison and her friend Brooke (Missy's fashion show bud) giggle.

"I've . . . uh. I've . . ."

He draws a circle in his grade book. "That's another zero for this week, Miss Thomas. With this and your missing critical essay, that brings your average down to a C minus."

My stomach knots up.

"Since Matt is out today, why don't you join Brooke and Allison?" Mr. Ludwig's wipes his parched lips. Gross. "Maybe you can learn from the two of them how to finish assignments."

Fabulous. I grab my notebook off Ludwig's desk and drag a chair next to Allison. Brooke glances at me and then looks at Allison, "Didn't know it was our job to provide remedial support."

Allison giggles.

With all the Matt craziness and everything else, I don't have the patience for this. I begin furiously scribbling in my notebook, attempting to (1) ignore them and (2) catch up on my Word-of-the-Day assignment.

"What? No witty comeback today, Teri?" Allison attempts to provoke me.

I practice my yoga breathing.

"Really, Teri? You don't have any brilliant one-liners you want to share with me?" Allison continues to mock me.

"I save them for people who are worth it. You know, people who can actually remember little things like other people's names from one day to the next." *Take that, Allison,* I think.

"Whatever," Allison says, pushing her circular glasses (used to make her look smarter) up the bridge of her nose. She turns to Brooke. "So, we had the best time last night."

"Where did you go?" Brooke asks, twisting her pen cap in her mouth as if it were a lollipop. "I was completely bummed that I had to miss out," she sighs.

I keep one eye on the doorway in case Matt walks by and write myself a note to finish up my Word of the Day.

"We hit Hyde with some up-and-coming actor who can't get enough of Vi," Allison giggles, keeping her iPhone underneath the desk so Mr. Ludwig doesn't catch her. "And get this, Matt met up with us after."

No wonder he ditched me for the bus. Must have had some three-B scoring to do. I sigh and pull my knees to my chest.

"Did you see Matt's fight this morning?" Brooke asks. "Nick totally had it coming."

"Yeah, I know." Allison adds, her eyes heavy after an all-nighter with Violet (or should I say, after a night of trying to get Vi to view her as more than an errand girl). "Matt's so random lately. I mean, he used to hang out a lot when he first came to B-Dub, but now he only comes out once in a while."

"I know what you mean," Brooke says. Leaning closer to Allison, she whispers, "But, you know, he's so hot, he can come out with me whenever he wants."

My ability to concentrate on Brooke and Allison's dissection of all-things-Matt is suspended by the appearance of Matt himself. He and Mr. Ludwig stand together in the front of the classroom. "Sure, Matt," I hear Mr. Ludwig say to him.

Mr. Ludwig opens up a binder and hands him a few papers. Then, he relays page numbers, which Matt swiftly scribbles in his English notebook.

It takes everything I have not to jump up and avalanche him with a billion questions. Never having had a parent permanently messed up, I can't imagine what Matt must be feeling after watching Nick diss someone in a wheelchair. But I want to know. And help.

"Thanks, Mr. L," Matt says, placing his notebook underneath his arm.

"Hey, Matt," Brooke yells from behind me. "Nick had it coming." She smiles, twisting her pen in her mouth like a lollipop.

Matt keeps his head down and walks out of the classroom. Immediately, I raise my hand.

"Yes, Taylor?"

I walk up to Mr. Ludwig and try not to be too obvious about my intentions. "Can I have a bathroom pass?"

Mr. Ludwig doesn't even look up as he scribbles across a pink pad. Ludwig is one of those male teachers who never hesitates to write out a hall pass to girls.

I grab the pass and sprint out the door.

Matt's about to cut the hallway corner when I yell, "Hey!!!"

Matt turns around and faces me.

"What happened?" I ask, when I reach him.

He leans against a locker and I notice his right knuckles are scabbed. "It was nothing. Nick's a prick."

"No, I mean what happened to you. Are you suspended?" All of a sudden, I'm noticing things about Matt that I never really noticed before. Like how he totally resembles an Abercrombie and Fitch model (a short one) when he leans against a locker.

"Two days. Then, the honor board will reinstate me after they read my essay about self-control." He glances behind him. "It doesn't matter." He turns back around and walks a few steps.

"Wait." I grab his arm. His school-store-bought sweatshirt has that worn-in, soft and comfy feeling, like a warm blanket on a cool beach night. "I thought it was really great what you did."

"I gotta go." He walks away. And this time, he doesn't turn back around.

As I'm heading back to English, a hand reaches out, grabs my arm, and pulls me into the empty janitor's closet. Zach. His warm breath hits my neck, sending shivers down my spine. *Guess it's time to finish up where we left off last night.*

"What are you doing?" I ask, still unwilling to be a three-B violator or a notch on the boys' three-B list. Even if Zach *was* pressured into doing it.

"I can't stop thinking about you." His lips inch toward mine. Reluctantly, I nudge him away.

"Zach, I can't."

"But, it's just me and you. No one will know."

I feel the cool doorknob.

I turn around and peck Zach on the cheek. "Thanks for thinking of me, but I have a basketball game to prep for." Then, I twist the knob, take a deep breath, and walk back to English.

fifty

Later, after practice, I rush home to shoot some hoops with my dad. I open the gate to my backyard, and as I close it behind me, I hear a soft and gravelly voice.

"Hey, Taylor." Zach smiles at me.

"Huh?" my legs feel as if they're stuck in mud. Zachary Murphy is here? In my backyard? Again? *Guess that little peck I gave him meant more than I thought.*

"Zach said he would help you with your press break, left-handed drives, and fade-away jump shots before Saturday's game against Richland." My dad comes up behind Zach, smacking his hand on his shoulder like they're old buds. "Wasn't it nice of Zach to stay after our workout to help you out?"

Zach's eye-sprinkles sparkle under the outside lights. "Since you need to prep and everything," he says.

My dad immediately takes control of the situation. "Okay." He bounces the ball to me. "Taylor, I'm going to pass the ball to you like it's the press break. Stand at the foul line. And Zach, stay on Taylor like glue. Real tight."

"Uh," I say, not sure what to do. I do need the practice,

and Dad and Zach went out of their way to do something nice for me. Plus, Zach's guidance would definitely help me prep for Saturday's game. The least I can do is smile and say thank you.

Zach feels for my waist and Dad snaps the ball into my palms. I think for a second: *What side I should fake? Should I go for a fade-away jump shot?*

I'm so caught up in the practice that I do not notice the car pull up to my house or the five girls that step out.

"Taylor, we're going to dinner and ..." Kylie, Missy, Jessica, Tamika, and Eva stop dead at my wrought-iron gate. All at once, their faces change from relaxed smiles to twisted disgust. Meanwhile, Zach's hand pushes against the small of my back. I turn around to look for my dad, so that he can help me explain what's going on, but he's behind a bush and completely out of their line of vision.

"What the hell are you doing?" Kylie screeches.

My stomach twists and turns. My palms go sweaty.

"That's messed up, Taylor," Tamika says, shaking her head.

One by one, my teammates glare at me, turn around, and storm away.

For a second, I'm so horrified, I can't move. But then I realize, I need to stop this. NOW. "Wait!" I yell and take off after them. But, it's too late. Missy's car backs up. Her headlights stream across my face as she makes the turn down my street.

My life is officially over.

fifty-one

This sucks. Big time. In the two hours since the girls caught me practicing with Zach, I've been de-friended by thirty-nine people. First, Kylie, then Missy, and now Tamika. Followed by bunch of others who aren't even on the team.

I click on Jessica's page. Kylie wrote, "What should we do about Taylor?" The question has turned into a major thread.

People have posted things like: "She's gotta go"; "She broke the rules"; "Rules are rules"; "You're going to lose on Sat if Tay doesn't play"; "Taylor's hot"; "Taylor rocks"; and "Taylor's the best b-ball player at BW." This is horrible. *How am I going to show my face in school tomorrow morning?*

As I read each comment, a flush crawls up my back. *What am I going to do?* I'm going to have to switch schools. Find another team to play for. But, what about Saturday? Our chance at a three-peat? What about the state playoffs?

I shut my laptop, snatch a basketball off my bedroom floor, fall back on my bed, and spin the ball in the air over and over and over and over. . . .

"Tay?"

Hannah catches me totally by surprise. I almost fall off my bed.

"Finally!" She lets out a deep breath and tosses a long, plastic garment bag on my pale blue comforter. "Where have you been? I've been texting you all day, and then I read that you're being kicked off the basketball team or something. What happened?" Hannah plops down next to me on my bed.

I take a deep breath. "My teammates caught me playing basketball with Zach."

"So what?" she says.

"No, Banana, you don't understand. *They caught me* in the backyard with Zach a couple hours ago."

"Ohmigod. I forgot. The three-B thing."

"Right."

"Did you hook up?"

"No." I lay back on my pillows and the plastic clothes protector crinkles underneath me. "He was helping me out with basketball."

"So, let me get this straight. The team thought you were hooking up with Zach again and you were just playing basketball?" Hannah wiggles her designs out from under me.

"Yup."

"Well, that's an easy fix."

"What do you mean it's easy? They want to kick me off the team. I mean, did you read everyone's posts tonight?"

"Just drop the nicey nice and explain what happened." Hannah pulls a super-short white silk dress out of the bag.

"What if they don't believe me?" I look up at her as she pulls out another design, this time a faux-fur vest with a caramel mini and a tiny, white "Skateboarding is Life" tee.

"This is what I was talking about the other day, Tay. Too nice. Walk right into school tomorrow and tell your teammates they completely overreacted."

"Yeah, that should go over well. Oh, and by the way, I'm tanking English."

"Why?" Hannah scrunches her nose.

"Because I've been so busy helping out with the fashion show, walking the runway, tutoring, worrying about guys, counseling friends, and playing basketball that I didn't have time for homework."

She looks at me. "Because you're too freaking nice. You really need to work on boundaries. They work wonders." She holds out the dress. "Now try this on so I can see if it needs any alterations."

I grab the dress and head toward my closet to change. I may have one remaining friend, a C-minus in English, a series of guys who are fawning over me only so that they can add my name to some stupid list, and a potentially permanent benching, but at least I can look pretty.

fifty-two

The next morning, I duck into the locker room for a breather before the first bell. All this stress is causing me to sweat so much that I've decided to start bringing extra shirts to school for non-fashion related purposes. But, popping into the locker room to change turns out to be far from my best decision.

"You slutbag!" Kylie shouts, lunging at me as soon as I step inside. Tamika grabs her from behind and pulls her onto a bench. "You screwed up three-B. You selfish skank!" she adds.

I swallow a lump the size of a basketball and freeze. Then, I take a deep breath and try to calm my trembling hands. Once I'm composed enough to speak, I opt for one-on-one defense. "Tamika," I say, hoping to appeal to her logical side.

She swivels around on the bench, turning her back to me. "We were just having a meeting, Taylor. One that you were not invited to."

Clearly, one-on-one didn't work, so instead I attempt a zone. "Look guys, I'm sorry." I scan my teammates. "My dad thought Zach could help me practice for Saturday's game. I didn't even know he was going to be there until I got home."

Missy crosses her arms. "Sure, we believe you." She rolls her eyes.

"You, of all people, should be the last one breaking the three-B rule considering you're the reason why we started all of this in the first place," Tamika finally speaks.

"But, I didn't do anything. I swear."

"So you want us to believe that you just happened to go home and Zach just happened to be in your backyard. Then, Kylie just happened to walk up when Zach was making out with you?" Missy says.

"Making out? We were practicing the press break play."

"Uh-huh." Kylie rolls her eyes. "I saw you making out with Zach seconds before the other girls walked up."

"Even I'm having a hard time believing you, Taylor," Jessica adds, crossing her arms.

"I'm serious. Look, you can ask my dad." I look at Kylie. By this time, my heart is pounding and my shirt is drenched with sweat. I take another deep breath. "As soon as you guys left, I went up to my room. Then, Zach left. I swear. Really, ask my dad. Or even Zach. I spent the rest of the night in my room, practicing for the fashion show." I swallow. "Look, I was wrong about Zach before. And I'm so sorry about that."

Tamika glances down at a paper in her hands and places it on the bench next to her. "Look, Taylor. This is difficult to say, but the team voted and we're going to Coach today to recommend that you get kicked off for lying to us and violating three-B."

"I'm sorry." A tear wells up in the corner of my eye, and I speedily wipe it away. This is basketball. I can't afford to be weak. I will not let them see me cry.

"How could you do this to the team the day before our biggest game of the year?" Tamika reprimands me.

"I, uh, I—" I shake my head and meander toward the door. I might as well be walking the plank.

fifty-three

"Mom," I whisper into my phone, wiping away a new set of tears with my free hand. I'm tucked away in a gymnasium closet outside the locker room.

"Honey, is everything all right?" she asks.

"No." the tears fall down my cheeks and my hands shake. "I need to talk to you."

Ambulance sirens sing in the background. "Mom, where are you?"

"I can't hear you. You're breaking up. What happened?" Mom answers.

"My teammates just kicked me off the basketball team."

"What, your roommates kicked you off the what?"

"My teammates want me off the basketball team, and they're going to tell Coach and my life is completely ruined."

Silence.

"Mom? Mom?" I shut my phone and attempt to dial again, but her phone goes right to voicemail. *Great, even my mom has abandoned me. Probably because she's off having some crazy hospital procedure that she doesn't want to tell me about, but still . . .*

I pull my legs to my chest and cry my heart out. My life is over. All my dreams. All the practices. All the hard work. I ruined the team. I ruined our chances at a three-peat. I ruined my big shot with the SoCal Suns. I ruined my life. Everything is ruined because I let a little guy-attention take over my entire existence.

A few minutes later, the door rips open, and I'm face-to-face with Christopher Phillips holding Brooke Lauder's hand and grinning ear-to-ear.

"Taylor." Chris's eyes light up.

I crawl out of the closet. "Uh, sorry, I didn't know you'd be . . . ." I slink forward, looking down.

"You can join us if you want." Chris winks.

I'm tempted to just get out of there, as fast as my legs will carry me, and leave Chris and Brooke to it (especially because she's horrible), but then I think about what Hannah said about me being a major People Pleaser. *Pretend you're driving to the basket.* I look back at Chris. "Why? So you can earn double points?"

Brooke looks at Chris than me, with a totally confused expression on her face. "What is she talking about?"

Chris shrugs and tugs her toward the closet.

I intervene. "I'm talking about the three-B game the guys are playing. It's all around school. The guys' basketball team and a couple other guys are racking up points based on how many girls they hook up with."

"Is this true?" Brooke rips her hand from Chris's.

"Uh . . . Uh . . ." Chris's face turns crimson.

"You. You. You're disgusting." Brooke's heeled boots tap across the gym floor.

Chris takes off after Brooke.

I'm pretty sure this day will go down in history as the day that Taylor Thomas got kicked off the basketball team and told off one of the most popular guys in school, thus transforming her reputation from "sweet, if insecure, basketball superstar" to "the kissless closet blocker." But I don't care. It felt good.

fifty-four

After securing the gym closet for myself (thereby costing Chris Phillips some serious points), I hang out in there for another period. Then I spend the rest of the afternoon ducking my teammates. Once the school day ends, I tiptoe toward the locker room, hoping the girls have found a way to forgive me. Zach waits outside the door, clad in his Beachwood warm-ups.

"Hey. Are you staying for my game?" he asks me. "Maybe we can go out afterward."

Before I can give Zach an "Are you kidding me?!?" I hear the sound of a basketball slamming into a wall. I turn to see Kylie charging toward us like an angry bull. The ball she threw ricochets off the wall and skims the top of Coach Jackson's head, who just happens to be walking out of the team room when all of this is going on. *Uh-oh.*

Coach Jackson's tired brown eyes dart from Kylie to me and then finally settle on Zach. "Kylie and Taylor, in my office, right now." Coach Jackson points behind her. "And you, Mister Murphy." She glares at Zach. "Don't go anywhere." Turning to the other team members, she announces, "The rest of you run until I return."

Groans echo throughout the gym.

"Thanks once again, Taylor," Tamika says, looking at me with disgust. "Come on girls."

My stomach is in knots as I trek toward our meeting. Kylie storms ahead of me. I mentally prepare myself for a major lashing from Coach.

When we arrive at her office, Coach Jackson pulls the wooden door open, and Kylie and I shuffle inside. Kylie parks herself in a chair in front of Coach's desk. Wanting to be as far away from this brouhaha as possible, I opt to stand by the door.

As I'm waiting for Coach to begin a (well-deserved) lecture, I stare at a poster of a hiker holding another guy by the arm. The two men stand on a copper cliff, and the word *Achievement* is written out in capital letters underneath. I concentrate on the poster and imagine myself standing there along with those guys. The image in my head shifts to playing basketball on the beach court. Then, I imagine being at home with my parents. Anywhere, but in this tiny office with crazy Kylie and a coach who is about to give me the tongue-lashing of the century.

Coach sits behind the desk and folds her hands in front of her. She looks at me. "Taylor, why don't you have a seat?" She points to the chair next to Kylie.

"I'm okay," I squeak, feeling a warm drip of sweat roll down my back.

"No, I don't think you are okay. In fact, I don't think either of you are okay. Whatever is going on has got to stop. We are not leaving this room until everything is sorted out." Coach clenches her thin lips together. "You two should be ashamed of yourselves. You let your own selfish problems get in the way of the team and our goals. At least now I know why we're playing like garbage." She mumbles something under her breath.

Chills shoot through my body. Coach is right. I'm *not* being a team player. Even if I don't mean to be selfish.

"All right. Taylor, let's start with you. What seems to be the problem?" Coach stares at me.

I shrug my shoulders.

Kylie swivels herself around to glare at me. "You don't know what's wrong! You hooked up with my boyfriend, pretended to be my friend, then broke the team rules. That's what's wrong."

The room is spinning, so I shut my eyes for a moment and grab the black metal bookshelf. *A Guide to Motivational Coaching* smacks on the floor. I bend down to pick up the book, trying to steady myself as my hand shakes, and end up bumping my head on the shelf in the process.

"This is all over a boy?" Coach leans back on her beige chair and looks at the ceiling. "For god's sake."

"Yes." Kylie lets out a dramatic breath. "Unfortunately, Taylor doesn't know what the definition of a teammate is." She glares at me.

Head **GAMES**

"What does Kylie mean by that statement, Taylor?" Coach asks. "I would hope that with the playoffs looming, we wouldn't be going out of our way to create problems." Her eyes narrow to tiny slits.

The tiny office begins to close in on me.

Kylie scrunches her miniscule, Jennifer Aniston nose and looks at Coach. "Then, when the team made a rule that we had to stay away from guys"—she pauses—"Taylor continued to hook up with Zachary behind our backs."

It's so hot in here. I clutch the front of my blue BMS tee, pulling at the collar. "That's not true," I squeak. "And you purposely wouldn't pass me the ball."

"Boys are not worth a teammate or a season, ladies. In fact, my old college coach used to say guys are like busses. Stand at the bus stop long enough and another one will show up. But your teammates are with you forever." Coach stands up, pushing away her chair. "I think there is only one way to solve this." Abruptly, she vacates the room.

I look around the office to find a tissue or something to wipe the sweat off my face.

"I still can't believe Zachary would want to hook up with a horse." Kylie snickers. "Forget what I said about you being an ugly duckling. You're not a duckling. You're just plain ugly. Inside and out."

What? No. I never want anyone to think of me like that. Even Kylie. I pride myself on being pretty on the inside.

Though I guess I have been talking back to people a lot lately . . . Ever since stuff with Zach took a turn.

Is that what happened to Kylie? Her relationship with Zach? She never used to be like this. She used to be nice and calm and sweet. Three years ago, she even took Charlotte Rosenberg, a guard from our AAU team, to a Taylor Swift concert after Charlotte's father died. And that was the kind of thing she did all the time. Well, not all the time. But, a lot. It's like Zach brings out this raging beast inside her. I mean, she's always been super aggressive on the court, and especially on the softball diamond, but everyone is a beast when they're playing their sport. *I just don't get it. What changed?*

Finally, Coach Jackson returns. Only this time, Zach trails behind her. I try to look at Coach directly, but she's fuzzy. I rub my eyes. Tiny black dots float across the room.

"I think Zach can settle this once and for all. Hopefully, we can then all move on, and maybe, just maybe, salvage the last twenty-four hours before our biggest game of the season." She points to an empty cherry wood chair in front of me and motions for Zach to sit.

Again, I tug at my collar (not only is it making me extra hot, but it seems to be constricting my breathing) and look up at the spinning ceiling.

"Since this mess involves you, Zach, we were hoping you could shed some light on it for us. So, tell me, Zach, what is going on?" Coach leans toward Zach.

Head **GAMES**

"Uh ..." Zach diverts his eyes from Coach's steely gaze. "Nothing?"

Bam. This time my slippery hand pushes a pile of books off the top of the bookshelf. Coach shoots me a death stare. "Sorry," I mutter and bend down to pick up the books, wishing I could squeeze into a hiding spot behind the bookcase.

Coach clears her throat. "Whatever is going on seems to be more than 'nothing.'"

"You broke up with me for one of my teammates!" Kylie points to Zach. "That's the worst thing in the world. I would never do that to you."

"What?" Zach faces Kylie.

"You went over to her house and hung out. Then, you broke up with me. For her. And just so you could score points for some stupid list." Kylie crosses her arms in front of her chest. Then she turns her attention to Coach. "Yeah, in case you were curious, the boys' basketball team and a couple other guys are making a list of all the girls they scored with, and whoever sucks face with the most girls wins."

"I don't think you want to do this here." Zach lowers his voice and hunches over like he wants to disappear.

"Yes, we are going to do this here." Kylie snaps her head in my direction. "Did you hook up with Zachary?"

I don't know what to say to that. My hand starts to shake again, and I tap my finger on my knee to make it look like I'm drumming.

"Uh . . ." I finally say.

Zach's gaze lingers on me.

Coach throws up her arms. "For god's sake."

Kylie uncrosses her arms and slides to the front of her chair. "I told you, Coach. She may look and act all innocent, but she's full of it."

Coach raises her eyebrows.

I stare at the locker room door.

"How do you think we can make this right?" Coach asks, staring at Kylie.

Kylie looks around the room. "Honestly, I don't know if we can. And because of that, we as a team propose that Taylor is kicked off the Wildcats for violating a team rule."

I can't breathe. I'm dying.

A knock interrupts my demise.

Hannah pokes her head in. "Can I see Taylor for a moment? She's helping me out in tonight's fashion show."

Coach glares at me, and I sheepishly turn around to face Hannah. "Uh, I'm kind of busy right now. I'll meet up with you soon."

Hannah takes in the severity of the scene in front of her and gives me one last pleading glance before leaving.

As soon as Hannah closes the door behind her, Coach picks up right where she left off. "I think I've heard enough."

This is it. The end of my basketball career.

But instead of incinerating me on the spot, Coach glares at Zach. "You, Romeo, can go. But you should know that I'm going to have to have a talk with your coach about all the extracurricular activities besides basketball your team is participating in."

Without a second glance, Zach dashes out of the room, clearly ecstatic to be free.

Coach shakes her head as he leaves. "I have a low tolerance for social lives interfering with our goals. Until the two of you stop placing your own needs in front of the team's, you're both done until further notice." She lets out a deep breath. "Okay, Kylie, you may go. Taylor, don't move a muscle." Coach vacates the room again.

As Kylie runs out the door behind Coach, she turns back to me for one final pronouncement: "You and Zachary have ruined my life."

fifty-five

A minute later, Coach returns. She sits down in front of me, looking just like she was informed that the Beachwood Academy higher ups cut the girls' basketball program indefinitely. "I have to say I'm very disappointed in you, Taylor. I never pegged you as the type to get involved in Beachwood drama."

I stare at my hands. She's right.

"I expect more out of you. In fact, I was hoping you would take on more of a leadership role this year."

I wipe my damp hands on my shorts.

"I realize that you're the most dedicated player out there. However, when we watched you play for Beachwood Middle, we didn't just notice your playing ability. We also recognized your leadership potential. But, to tell you the truth, I haven't seen you realize that potential since joining us at the high school level."

I look up at Coach. Her lips are pursed. "I'm sorry," I say. Between missing out on the Suns opportunity and being a part of all this boy drama, I feel like I just keeping letting people down. "I promise this won't happen again."

"Consider this a lesson learned. You have too much to lose. Very soon, these Beachwood boys are going to seem like ancient history. I would hate to see inconsequential issues get in the way of your very bright future." Coach stands up. "I want you to stay in here for a few more minutes and think about what you could have done to avoid this situation. Meanwhile, I'm going to meet with your teammates to determine the proper punishment for both you and Kylie." She walks out the door.

I spend the next ten minutes thinking hard and looking at pictures of past championship teams. Quickly, I resolve that I will be like those girls. I will be part of a championship team. I will be a leader. I will make the SoCal Suns. I will play basketball in college. And I won't let anything get in my way. Ever again.

I'm about to leave when Tamika walks into the office.

Oh, no. She must be here to deliver my punishment. My stomach flips.

Tamika sits down in Kylie's seat. "As you know, Coach just met with the team. She's giving us some time to decide what should happen to you and Kylie."

I slump back down in the chair. "I'm so sorry, Tamika. I should have put the team first. I'll do anything to make it up to you guys."

"Actually after thinking through everything, we as a team have decided to ask Coach to keep you and to kick Kylie off the team."

"What?" I look up at Tamika, totally stunned.

"Let's be honest, Kylie's main sport is softball. And anyway, she's the one who started all the drama." Tamika crosses her arms.

"Well, there was more to it than—"

"Taylor, that's very nice of you to try to defend her, and don't think that you're totally off the hook, but let's look at all the facts. One, she and Zach were broken up; two, it's not the first time she's done this; and three, we originally based your being kicked off the team on information Kylie gave us. And how do we know she was even telling the truth?" Tamika uncrosses her arms and places her hands on her hips. "Plus, tomorrow's game against Richland is do or die. And we need you to win more than we need her."

Although their offer is tempting, I think about what Coach said about not being selfish.

"We're going to tell Coach in a few minutes, but I wanted to let you know before the hysterics start." Tamika turns around to walk out the door.

"Wait," I say, standing up. "You can't do that."

Tamika stops. "What? I thought you'd be happy. No more Kylie. No more drama."

"We're a team, Tamika. We can't just turn our backs on a teammate."

Tamika's mouth hangs open. "Seriously?"

"Kylie and I can work together. I just know that when

Head GAMES

the time comes, we can put this stuff aside for the sake of the team."

"You sure you're not just being nice?" Tamika eyes me suspiciously. "Because this is about making the playoffs. Not about being nice."

"Positive." I stand up straighter. "This is the way it has to be."

fifty-six

After barely keeping my spot on the team, I'm totally beat. Even though I've begun to "relish the awesomeness of my inner fashionista" (to quote Hannah's fashion show mantra), the absolute last thing I want to do is hang out in heels with Missy, Violet, and the rest of the Beachwood babes. But, even after the basketball fiasco, I have no choice but to strap on my big girl heels and fashion show it up. I did promise poor, hobbling Hannah after all.

Backstage at the fashion show, things are crazy. Between the designers frantically running around and the models receiving last minute touch ups to their hair and makeup, it's an absolute madhouse. Not wanting to get in anyone's way, I stay in the back corner and wait for Hannah to come find me.

"There you are!" Hannah calls out, noticing me from across the room. She slowly makes her way through the throngs of girls, leaning on her right crutch and pushing along a clothing rack holding a garment bag with her left. "I thought you left."

"Nope. Still here." I let out a deep breath.

Hannah unzips the hanging garment bag to reveal the vest, paint-splattered T-shirt, and mini. Then she opens up another cover to expose the ivory silk dress. The looks may be way different, but only one word comes to mind: *amazing*.

"So, are you ready?" Hannah asks, her eyes wide. She's totally in her element.

"As ready as I'll ever be." And I am. I'm so proud to be Hannah's model.

"Good." She adjusts the fur vest on the hanger. "So. What are you going to do now that you discovered your two main guys are three-B players?"

"What are you talking about 'two guys'?"

"Matt and Zach."

"Matt isn't my main guy." I still can't believe I opened up to him on our beach walk after I knew he was participating in the three-B list. *Stupid. Stupid. Stupid.*

"Are you sure about that? You looked pretty freaked out after his fight. That's all you talked about *all* day."

"We're friends."

"Friends with benies." Hannah winks. "And if you guys are so-called friends, then, why is he here?"

What?!? I turn around and am face-to-face with a Beachwood Lacrosse hat.

"Taylor." Matt stands there, holding a bundle of white daisies. "I just wanted to wish you good luck."

Huh? Flowers? Really? Is that the best he can do? How about apologizing for the three-B list? I want to believe that he's genuine. Really, I do. But first Zach, now Matt? Why does every guy on the list think I'm just going to forget everything and let them take advantage of me? Do I have "dumb" stamped across my forehead? This is just some last minute ploy for more points.

But I'm not going to fall for it. Once and for all, I'll show Hannah that I too can put up boundaries.

I grab the daisies off Matt and dump them in the garbage can behind me. Well, at least what I thought was a garbage can. Turns out it was really some sort of suitcase. Philippe, the hairdresser, shoots me a dirty look. I pick up the flowers, say a quick sorry, and toss them on the floor to make sure that the full effect is not lost on Matt. Then, I turn my back to him, making sure I don't allow the perfect curvature of his cute butt to change my mind.

Head GAMES

"Stay still," Philippe says a few minutes later, as he fluffs a brown mop of my curls. Turns out a curling iron plus my natural frizz does not equal the *très merveilleux* look he was going for.

"Ten minutes till showtime." Mrs. Sealer sashays through the crowd.

"Flip," Philippe says.

"Huh?" I watch Missy, who is getting fake eyelashes pasted on in the seat next to mine, glare at me through my reflection in the mirror.

"Yur head. Flip eet upside down," he says with a French accent.

I lean forward.

"Perrrrfek." He moves a few pieces of hair around and finishes with a spray.

"Violet, take your spot!" Mrs. Sealer shouts above the din.

"Come on, Tay." Hannah yanks me off the seat. I grab my ruby heels as she shuffles me along. Despite her injury, Hannah is remarkably strong when she wants to be.

"Here. Put this on," she instructs.

"In front of everyone?" The idea of all these people watching me change is utterly horrifying.

"This is backstage at a fashion show. Of course, you're changing in front of everyone! Now put this on. You're up in one minute. No time to lose!"

I sigh and maneuver Hannah directly in front of me in a last ditch attempt to salvage my dignity. Even though she barely covers me, I turn around, slide off my practice clothes, and slip into the ivory dress.

Hannah swiftly makes a few last-minute adjustments. Then, she swings backward on her crutches to admire her handiwork. "Perfect! You look stunning, Tay!" She wipes away a tear. "Seriously, you look gorgeous. Come here. You need to see this," she says, pointing to a mirror.

Ohmigod. Kylie was right. I'm a swan. While gazing at myself in the mirror, I spin around just like they do in the movies, noticing how my eyes pop just like Selena Gomez's. Then, I finger the silk of the dress and am wowed by how perfectly it falls against my body. I tousle my light brown hair, which has somehow miraculously ceased being frizzy, and am struck by how it falls in soft waves below my shoulders. I kind of actually resemble a model. *Is this really me?*

"Gorgeous!" Philipe stops in front of me, gasps, and clasps his hand in front of his mouth.

"Next up, Taylor Thomas for Banana Fad," Helen Tierra, a local fashion designer with her own reality show, announces from her perch in the auditorium.

Hannah nudges me forward, and I step out past the hanging curtains onto the red-carpeted catwalk. Surrounded by white lights and an enormous crowd, and fueled by the soft beat of some unnamed techno song, I jut my hips out and sashay just like I've been practicing.

"Hannah Montgomery of Banana Fad has been designing for five years. She's a premier skateboarder who loves to mix punk, alternative, and high fashion. This is her first appearance at the Beachwood Spring Fashion Show," Helen Tierra continues. *Hannah must be freaking out that one of her design idols is announcing her line.* "Taylor Thomas is modeling Banana Fad's designs this evening. Taylor is the star center on the basketball court and, from the looks of it, a natural model."

Did Helen Tierra just call me a natural model? My heels wobble a bit, but I play it off just like the models I've been studying on *America's Next Top Model.*

As I'm about to reach the end of the runway and do my turn, hip thrust, turn, hip thrust, I spot Zach in the crowd. He winks at me and nods his head. Standing next to him is another senior, Matthew Connelly, a forward on the basketball team and football stud known to club with Violet on occasion.

Ohmigod.

Matt Connelly. I had the wrong Matt. Matt Connelly is the "Matt" on the three-B list.

I lose my breath, forget to turn, and step right off the edge of the runway.

fifty-eight

"Taylor, your blood work is normal. And I'm not seeing anything unusual on the CAT Scan," says Dr. Nelson, a brunette emergency room doctor who looks like the fourth Kardashian sister. She maneuvers her hand underneath my gray gown and unhooks the probes stuck to my flat chest.

She glances at my dad, who has just removed his yellow L.A. Sparks hat and is now wiping his forehead. "Just keep an eye on Taylor this evening," she instructs. "She's still a bit banged up from the fall." She scribbles something on a clipboard. As she moves around the curtained-off patient room, I catch sight of her three-inch coal sling-backs, and admire how effortlessly she walks. No ruby-red heel wobbles for her.

"Taylor has an important basketball game coming up tomorrow. Do you think she'll be able to play?" my dad asks, moving to the edge of his seat.

"I don't see why not. The tachycardia noted in the ambulance was caused from stress. And everything else looks normal." Dr. Nelson glances at me. "But I have to ask, have you been under a lot of stress lately, Taylor?"

I think back over the last couple of weeks—the homework, the tutoring, Hannah, the fashion show, three-B, basketball, my teammates, the Suns, Zach, Matt . . . "Uh. Yeah," I say. I'm tempted to tell her that "a lot of stress" is a major understatement.

Dr. Nelson shakes her head, knowingly. "I have some great literature on how to deal with stress. I'll include it with your discharge instructions."

"Thanks," I say, just wanting to leave the ER and get on with my life.

Dr. Nelson parts the curtain and steps out of the room.

For the first few seconds after she leaves, Dad and I sit in silence. I stare at my long, dangling legs until I can't take it any longer. "Where's Mom?" I ask. "Why isn't she here with me?"

My dad lets out a deep breath. "I guess I should tell you, Spider. She's here."

"What?" My head snaps in his direction. "She's in the hospital?"

Dad scoots farther forward on his chair and grabs my hand. I can't remember the last time my dad held my hand, except maybe to pull me to run faster or to show me how to execute a basketball move. *This must be seriously bad.* "Mom is on her way down. She said she'll meet us in the waiting area."

"Okay, but what's wrong with her?"

Before my dad can answer, Dr. Nelson pulls open the curtain. "Here's my card and Taylor's discharge instructions."

She hands the papers to my dad. "Again, make sure she takes it easy tonight, and if she's feeling good tomorrow, I don't see any reason why she can't play."

As she's talking, I'm distracted by the sight of a short, stocky guy in a royal blue hoodie pushing a man in a wheelchair. Beside him is a nurse rolling an IV pole and clutching a thick binder.

I stand up, pull the curtain back a bit, and peek out. *It really is Matt.* There's no mistaking it. Suddenly, he and the nurse stop in the middle of the emergency room floor, apparently to adjust his father's oxygen tank. As the nurse is playing around with the tubes, Matt squats down next to the wheelchair and pats his dad's hand. I can't help but notice how tenderly he speaks to him. No wonder Matt defended Patrick. How could he not have?

My dad steps in front of me, blocking my view. "Ready to see Mom?"

"I'll meet you in the waiting room. I need to get changed first. And I think I might also stop at the bathroom."

"Okay, Spider. Just try to move as fast as possible. We need to finish our conversation."

As soon as Dad walks away, I slide across the emergency room floor in my stocking feet. Although I'm aching to know what the story is with my mom, I can't leave the hospital without first speaking to Matt.

"Matt!" I call out. He turns around to face me, a shocked expression on his face. I remember that I'm wearing a partially see-through hospital gown and pull it tighter, crossing my arms in front of my chest so that no body parts are visible.

"Taylor, what are you doing here?" Matt steps away from his father, pulling me into a partitioned room.

"Uh . . . long story. Tell you later if you really wanna know." I feel my face flush. "Look, I'm just going to throw this out there. Am I a bonus babe to you?"

Matt's face twists like he's just eaten sour candy. "A what?"

"A bonus babe."

"Taylor, I don't know what you're talking about," Matt answers.

"Good." I smile. And right there, in my pink-and-gray hospital gown, I decide to make things right. "Sorry about the daisies. Do you still want to go to that poetry slam after my game tomorrow?"

Matt opens his mouth to reply but is cut short by an unwelcome visitor.

"Hey, Tumbling Tay Tay. How's your butt?" Violet walks up to us, still in stage makeup, and links her arm with Matt's. "You should have seen Tay take a dive at the fashion show.

I roll my eyes.

"Are you okay?" Matt asks.

Before I can answer him, Violet butts in.

"Eh. She's fine." Violet waves off my injury. She turns toward Matt. "Is your dad ready?"

Matt glances in my direction. "Well, uh . . . yeah, I think so."

"Awesome!" Violet replies. She links arms with him again and pulls him away. Matt looks back at me, mouths "sorry," and then quickens his pace to match Violet's.

What was I thinking? Matt Moore is taken. I turn around and slide back to my room.

fifty-nine

"Taylor!" My dad finds me as I emerge from the hospital room, having just finished changing back into my (now ripped) silk dress. "What's taking so long? Your mother and I have been waiting for you."

Yikes. I was so caught up thinking about my abridged conversation with Matt, I almost forgot Mom is in the hospital. I sprint toward the waiting room.

Upon seeing me materialize, my mom throws her arms open for a hug. "Sweetheart," she says. "I was so worried about you."

She wraps her arms around me and squeezes hard.

A tear rolls down my cheek.

"Mom," I say, breathing in her familiar Coco Channel perfume. "What's going on? Are you sick? I didn't want to ask Dad why you weren't in the ER with me, but then I just had to know because I've hardly seen you lately and I've been so worried. And it seems like something really bad is going on, but no one will tell me, and I don't know why. And if you have a problem, you should let me help. I'm a good listener and I'll be there for you. And I love you so much, but I'm just so worried." I blurt out all at once.

She lets me go, and I take a good look at her. Her skin is pasty and she's wearing a blue hospital band around her wrist.

She silently looks up at Dad.

"Come on, what is it?" I ask, unable to hold in my concern any longer.

Mom lets out a deep breath and her turquoise eyes meet mine. "Remember how I told you that Daddy and I always wanted to give you a brother or a sister, but it just wasn't meant to be?"

I nod, remembering the day they finally let me expand my room.

"Now that you're old enough, I can share with you what happened. After Daddy and I had you, we tried to get pregnant almost every day for ten years. We tried everything: specialists, in-vitro fertilization, you name it. But nothing worked. So, a few years ago, we gave up hope."

"I'm sorry, Mom." I squeeze her hand.

She grins and squeezes back. Then, she looks up at my dad and back at me. "Well, I guess we gave up too soon. Because, well . . . I'm pregnant."

sixty

"I knew you'd be upset," my mom says as I play with my hospital bracelet.

"I'm not upset," I insist.

"You sure?" my dad asks.

"I'm okay. I just wish you guys told me sooner." I give my mom another hug. "I was really freaking out about you."

"Aw, honey." She returns to hand-squeezing position, only now both hands are involved. "Daddy and I didn't tell you because I wasn't sure if the pregnancy would take. We've lost so many pregnancies over the years that we didn't want to get your hopes up. And with all these appointments and all the stuff they're pumping me with, I've been so tired and sick all the time. It just never seemed like the right time to tell you. Eventually, we just decided to wait until after the first trimester."

"You should have told me," I repeat.

"You're probably right, sweetie. Keeping the pregnancy a secret probably only made things worse. But your dad and I were so concerned about how this pregnancy was going to affect you."

"You didn't need to worry, Mom. I'm so happy for you

guys." I muster up the biggest smile I can manage, which, considering my recent tumble off the runway and Violet's upstaging me in front of Matt, is a major feat.

"But, what about you, honey? How do you feel about it?" she asks.

"I'm excited. Now Dad will have someone else to play basketball with." I force myself to continue smiling. "And we can learn from my mistakes, so they'll end up way better than me."

"What? What mistakes are you talking about, Taylor? You've done so many amazing things. We're so unbelievably proud of the woman you're becoming," my mom says, twirling a piece of my hair around her finger.

"On and off the court," my dad pipes up.

"What do you mean, on the court, dad? I totally messed up the Suns audition."

"Oh, Spider, don't worry about it. You'll get another shot at the Suns," my dad replies.

"I promise, Dad, I won't ever let you down again." I look at him, my eyes wide.

"What are you talking about? How'd you let me down?" he asks.

"You gave up on your basketball career because of me. And you've put so much time and effort into my game. The least I can do is show up."

"Is that what you think?" my dad asks, taking off his hat and scratching his head.

"Yeah." I squirm around in the silk dress. "I see how you look when you're watching basketball games. Like you want to be out there, shooting with the best of them. But you can't. Because you gave it up. Because of me."

"I gave up basketball because it was time," he replies.

"But you quit right before I was born...."

"Like I said, because it was time. Your mother and I decided that that would be my last year playing regardless. And it just happened that we got pregnant. And anyway, everything worked out for the best. I would never give up all the time I've spent with you, Spider. You and your mom mean more to me than basketball ever did." He wraps one arm around my mom's shoulders and the other around mine. "Yes, I loved the feeling of being out there on the court, with the clock running down and the fans cheering. But that's nothing compared to the joy I experience watching you grow and mature. You're my life now, Spider. You, your mom, and this baby. And I wouldn't change it. Not for the world."

sixty-one

As I push open the heavy, wooden locker room door early the next morning, I hear sobs. Deep, heaving sobs. I pick up my pace and turn the corner.

I'm greeted by a mane of perfect, shiny, curly blonde hair, beneath which are bloodshot eyes. Kylie.

"Are you okay?" I ask, forgetting for a moment that she hates me.

"I'm fine," Kylie says as she wipes away the tears with the back of her sweater sleeves. "I'm just here to get my stuff."

For a moment, she resembles the Kylie I remember before she turned crazy.

"Of all people, I really don't need *you* seeing me like this," she says, letting out another sob. "I never want *anyone* to see me like this."

"I'm not here to judge you, Kylie." I sit down next to her on the bench. "Remember, we used to be friends."

"Used to," Kylie reiterates. "Really, Taylor. No offense, but you're the last person I want to talk to right now." Kylie continues to dab her eyes with her beautiful merino wool sleeves until I can't take it anymore. I run to the nearest girls' bathroom, which fortunately is deserted since it's early Saturday morning, grab a bunch of tissues, and jog back to Kylie's side. When I hand her the tissues, she looks at me, quizzically, as if deciding what kind of message accepting them would send. She sniffles some more and I shove them at her. I'm not accepting no for an answer. Finally, she takes them. I smile at her. It doesn't matter to me that she doesn't offer a thank you. At least she's using them.

We sit in silence for a while. The only sounds are Kylie's sniffles and the *tick tock, tick tock* of the Wildcat clock hanging above the lockers.

After this goes on for some time, I turn to her. "Look, if you're off the team, then I quit."

She looks at me and squints. "You don't mean that."

"I'm serious. I talked to Tamika yesterday. I'm not playing today unless you're out there with me."

Kylie just sits there. Silent.

I continue regardless. "We're a team. And we're going to win as a team."

Kylie's still silent.

"And even if by some stroke of fate we manage to win without you, which I seriously doubt would ever happen, it wouldn't mean anything. Not unless you're a part of it."

Again, Kylie doesn't say a word.

"Anyway, I've been wondering something for a while now. Why didn't you destroy me like you did Chloe?" I ask, figuring the question will at least break the torturous silence hovering over us.

She looks at me with her bloodshot eyes. "Believe me, I wanted to." Then, she glances down at her hands. "I even found the perfect picture on the Internet of a girl who looked exactly like you hooking up with two girls and everything. But, after I heard Zachary hung out with you, I knew it wasn't the girl this time, it was him." She dabs her eyes again. "I mean, I've known you my whole life. Even if you liked Zachary, you still wouldn't make a move on him because you're too nice."

So, that's why she never perceived me as a real threat before all this started. And all this time I thought it was because of my height.

"You're not like everyone else," Kylie continues. "I think that's why it upset me so much when I heard about the two of you. Because once he went after you, I knew what was really up."

Although the compliment is kind of backhanded (and Kylie's attitude throughout this whole thing doesn't exactly make me feel any better about it), I decide to take it as it was intended. "Thank you for believing in me," I say.

Kylie nods. "Well, since you're here and everything, you might as well tell me. What really went on between you and Zachary?"

I scoot down the bench just in case hearing what happened aloud makes her decide to grab me by the neck or something. "At first, I ran into him at the beach courts. And we had a good time playing one-on-one together, so he stopped by my house and we played some more."

"Yeah, right."

"No, that's how it started. Basketball. Then, he texted me and we hung out together."

Kylie crosses her arms in front of her chest. "Did he kiss you?"

"Yeah." I cringe, sliding farther away from Kylie.

"Was it last Sunday night?"

I nod.

"I knew it. He's such a liar. He actually came over to my house that night. I'm so stupid." She sniffles again.

"Kylie, you're not stupid," I say. "It's not like our team came up with the three-B rule just because of you. Seems to me that guys can turn all of us into mush."

Kylie turns to face me, red splotches covering her face. "Yeah, three-B. That was genius. Did you hear what ended up happening with the guys' three-B list? The points thing, I mean. Zachary actually won. Translated: He's like the biggest player at our school. I hate him." She pounds the bench with her fist.

"You know, Kylie, you could have any guy you wanted." I slide back in her direction.

"Right now, I just want to stop doing this crazy thing with Zachary." She takes a deep breath.

I shrug my shoulders. "You just like Zach. It's hard to help who you like." I reach my arm across Kylie's shoulders to give her a squeeze of support. As I'm doing so, I can't help but think back to sleepovers during AAU tournaments when I would hear Kylie sniffling late at night, and she would swear it was just allergies. "I'm sorry for everything, Kylie."

"Me too. Let's just cut the drama and kick some butt. And not yours this time, Richland's." The last word comes out with some serious attitude. Kylie's back.

sixty-two

"Hey, guys! I want you to know that Kylie and I worked everything out. For real this time," I say as I jog over to join my teammates at the center of the gym.

Kylie walks over to us. "Yup. The whole thing is over. Taylor didn't hook up with Zachary after we signed the three-B contract, so we're cool."

My teammates look up at Kylie as if she just announced she's really a dude.

"Today is too important," I say. "Kylie and I will never put anything in front of the team again."

"Really?" Missy asks.

"Yeah, basketball means too much to us to let stupid stuff get in the way. And this is our chance to get a playoff bid *and* finally three-peat!" I exclaim.

Tamika giggles. "Yeah, but are you still sore from yesterday's stage dive?" she asks.

The ice melts as the rest of my teammates break into laughter.

"A little bit," I reply. "But don't think it'll get in the way of my crushing Rodriguez and the rest of Richland today."

"It better not!" Tamika jokes.

"Sooooo, Taylor, we heard that other than your falling episode, you did a really great job at the show," Jessica says.

"Yeah, check this out." Eva turns her iPhone horizontal and clicks the screen. A pic of me in the ivory dress walking the runway appears.

"Wow, check out Taylor," Zoe says, grabbing the phone. "She's on fire!"

"You look amazing." Abby grins, nudging me with her elbow.

I stare at the pic. *Is that girl with the cascading chestnut curls, pouty lips, and almond eyes, really me?*

In a stroke of perfect timing, Hannah hobbles over to the team. "What's all this fuss about?" she asks. "Is everyone congratulating my model?"

"Kind of," I reply. "But you're the one who really deserves some major congrats."

"Yeah, Hannah," Jessica says. "Your designs are unbelievable."

"Aren't they?" I say, enveloping her in a hug.

"Thanks, Tay. Your walk certainly made my fashions memorable." She grins. "Did you get my get-well flowers?"

"Yeah," I say. "And I made you a thank you." I dig into my bag and hand Hannah the card. It reads: "Although I'm making a concerted effort to showcase my inner beast from time to time, I still think that there are certain occasions that call for politeness."

"Tay, you really are the sweetest!" Hannah smiles. "Though, let's face it, you're still sort of a klutz in heels. A gorgeous klutz, but a klutz." She then opens up her bag to throw the thank you card inside, and as she's doing so, notices that her phone is buzzing. She glances at it and shouts, "Oh. My. God."

"What happened?" Jessica asks.

"I just got a text from my sister," Hannah answers.

"Is she having a fashion disaster or did Daddy say no?" Kylie giggles.

"No, I think it turns out that—surprise, surprise—she actually has a heart," Hannah announces.

"No! Violet? *Really*?" I joke.

She holds up her phone. "No, really. She said she's too busy to pick me up after the game because she'll be at a rehab center."

"A rehab center?" Missy asks. "Who's in rehab?"

"Apparently, it's Matt Moore's dad." Hannah sucks in a dramatic breath. "I just found out that my sister pulled some strings and got a few of my dad's contacts to donate money so that he could be set up there."

"Why on earth would she do that?" Kylie asks.

"I don't know, but I'm guessing it has something to do with the magazine interview she has scheduled for today about her work as a good Samaritan." Hannah chuckles.

"And all this time I thought Violet was hooking up with Matt," I say, under my breath.

"I didn't even know Matt's dad was an alcoholic," Zoe says.

"Me neither." Abby adds.

Everyone looks at me.

"Did you?" Hannah asks.

"It's a rehabilitation center for sick people. Matt's dad is in a wheelchair," I answer.

"Oh. No wonder he fought Nick the other day," Jessica says. "That's horrible."

"Did you know my sister was doing this?" Hannah asks.

"Not exactly," I reply, feeling the butterflies flutter in my stomach. All I can think is: *Violet was in it for the fame. She and Matt were never an item. And best of all, he's single!*

sixty-three

The Beachwood stands are filling up faster than the butterflies are taking residence in my stomach. I'm surprised to spot the guys' team in the stands, especially with three-B logos painted on their chests. But I quickly turn away, refusing to make eye contact. Today my focus is on Richland. No distractions.

"Girls, bring it in!" Coach Jackson calls out. She and Coach Martie are standing by the sidelines.

We hustle over and I breathe in deeply, attempting to stay calm.

"This is it." Coach Jackson surveys the team, making eye contact with each player. "When we win today, we qualify for the playoffs and earn our three-peat." Coach pulls out her clipboard. "It's time to show Southern California that BW is still number one."

"Stay tough today. Remember mental toughness and teamwork win championships," Coach Martie adds.

Then both coaches turn around and meet the opposing coaches in the middle of the court for the coin toss.

Tamika gives us a pep talk of her own. "Forget about last week. Let's just give it one hundred percent. Think about everything we've sacrificed. Every lap we ran. Every drill. The three-B's. Today's our day. Let's do it." We pile our hands in the middle of the circle. "Team on three. Ready, one, two, three."

We shout, "Team!"

After the team is announced and the "Star Spangled Banner" plays, one by one my teammates jog onto the court. Meanwhile, Kylie and I each take a seat on the bench. Coach decided that with all the drama, it wouldn't be fair for us to start. Still, we're at the edge of our seats, super anxious to get into the game.

"Be ready to go in." Coach Jackson glances at us.

We smile at each other. We're going to get to some court time after all.

I watch Missy take my spot at center court as Richland's center, Nikki Rodriguez, glares at her. I think Rodriguez is even bigger than she was last Friday. If that's even possible.

I shift in my seat. It should be me out there. Rodriguez has at least eight inches on Missy.

"Is everybody ready?" The ref points to the players, then bends at the knees. "Here we go!" He tosses the ball into the air.

Rodriguez easily tips the ball back to her waiting guard. The guard snatches the ball, and Rodriguez sprints down the court toward her basket. Missy takes off behind Rodriguez, but the guard launches the ball into Rodriguez's open hands.

Head **GAMES**

She easily lays it right into the net, leaving Missy trailing behind.

"Missy! Get into better position!" Martie screams from the sideline.

After Rodriguez easily scores eight more points, Coach Jackson looks at us. "Taylor, Kylie, go in."

When the ref blows the whistle a minute later as the ball rolls out of bounds, Missy and I slap hands. She looks relieved to leave the center position.

"Come on, Taylor!" I recognize my dad's voice bellowing from the crowd.

Kylie takes the ball out of bounds and, like Coach predicted, Richland is pressing hard and tough.

I make my way to my spot on the foul line. Rodriguez is nasty, and our one-on-ones become shoving matches for position. Hannah's right. On the court, I'm the opposite of nice.

"Calm down, girls." The ref eyes us.

"Press break eleven!" Kylie calls from her spot as guard. She darts around the court like an ornery puppy as Richland defends us full court and tight.

Kylie bounce passes the ball to our strong forward, Eva. She catches it and swings around, jabbing her elbows for position. Eva then returns the ball to Kylie who uses Tamika as a pick.

Jessica runs toward me for the pick. She stands in front of the Richland guard with her arms across her chest.

I run at Jessica. She picks off Rodriguez. Rodriguez sends Jessica sliding toward the sideline on her butt. Ouch.

Meanwhile, Kylie launches the ball my way and I set up.

After I release, I stand for a moment and watch the ball swish through the net. This basket is sweeter than ever.

"You got lucky," Rodriguez says as she runs past me. "And remember, I'll be the one wearing the purple and yellow this summer."

I look at Rodriguez and chuckle. She can try to provoke me all she wants. This three-peat is all ours.

sixty-four

With five minutes left, we go back and forth with Richland like a seesaw. First, they're up by two. Then we're up by two. It's crazy.

During a time out, Coach grabs a white clipboard and begins to scribble circles and squares all over it. "Okay. It's time for the full-court press," she announces, huddling next to me.

Fireworks rip through my stomach. Something about full-court defense makes me flustered. Not tonight. Not now.

"Jessica, you stay on number two."

Jessica nods and squirts water into her open mouth. Her ponytail is saturated with sweat.

"Eva, I want you to trail twenty-one."

Eva nods, adjusting her headband.

"And Tamika, on number forty-four."

Tamika smiles and glances over at Richland's huddle.

"Kylie, you're on the guard tight. And Taylor, you stay with Rodriguez. Let's deny the ball and trap. Give it everything you got."

I shake out my hands and jog in place. *Focus. Focus.*

The buzzer sounds to signal the end of the time-out. The gym is super quiet.

"One, two, three, team!" we shout.

We jog out onto the court. Rodriguez smirks at me as their guard grabs the ball. "You gonna trip and fall today, Thomas?"

"Whatever, Nikki." I roll my eyes. "You so wish you were runway material."

Rodriguez laughs. "I'm SoCal material." Then, she hangs out by the end line, watching and waiting. I know what she's doing. She thinks she can use her speed to beat me to the basket. I take a couple steps back and turn my body so I'm ready for a sprint.

The ref tweets his whistle and hands the ball to the guard. Just as expected, Nikki takes off toward the basket. But I'm two steps ahead of her. I stick to her, cutting off the launch pass at the last second to grab the ball. Rodriguez flies past me, crashing into the wall, shocked the ball isn't in her hands.

Quickly, I take off toward the basket, leaving Richland's guard no choice but to hack me in the lane. After almost a year of weight training with a personal trainer, I'm strong enough to get murdered under the basket and still easily lay the ball up into the net. And that's what I do just as the ref blows his whistle.

"One-four, foul, basket counts, one," the ref signals to the center table. The crowd hoots and cheers. My mom and dad are on their feet, clapping wildly. My teammates surround me.

At this point, we're up by two. If I sink this basket, they're forced to shoot a three. If I don't sink this, then an easy basket could tie and put us into overtime. I make my way to the foul line, taking in long, fluid breaths, calming my nerves.

The two teams line up as I set up behind the foul line. The ref stands inside the paint and holds the ball. He does a quick position check and tosses me the ball for the foul shot.

As I bounce the basketball, it echoes through the silent gym. I take a deep breath and stare at the far rim, like I always do when I'm shooting foul shots. Deep breath. Bounce again. I bend down and set up for the shot.

"You stink!" a guy from Richland's side yells.

"Don't choke like you did last night," someone else adds.

I grin and release, waving at the ball as it sails towards the basket.

Swish.

Again, the crowd goes nuts and my teammates huddle around me. Richland's guard takes the ball outside the line, and I stick to Rodriguez like gum on a shoe. With twenty seconds left, our full-court press is on again. Kylie does jumping jacks, attempting to stop the guard from in-bounding the ball. The ref stands next to Richland's guard, counting down the seconds with his hands.

Finally, the Richland guard finds Rodriguez, who breaks away from me with her speed and footwork. The entire gym is on their feet. Rodriguez is known for her three. I stay tight on her, hoping I can stop her dribble. But, she breaks right and I give her a few steps.

"Foul her," Coach Jackson calls.

I stand in front of Rodriguez and realize I'm better off fouling her before she sets up for the three. Before she lifts her arms to shoot. I slam into her hard.

The ref blows his whistle. "Foul, number four, one and one."

"That's three shots. She was shooting a three!" the Richland coach shouts from their side, throwing a fit. She throws down her clipboard in a huff. White pieces of paper scatter across Richland's side.

The ref ignores the craziness and returns to the line. Rodriguez sets up at her basket. She finds her spot behind the line, and I glance at the clock. Five seconds. Most likely, she'll sink the first one. Then she'll bang the second one off the backboard, hoping someone will grab the rebound and sink the shot for the tie.

The gym is silent. I stare at Rodriguez as she bounces the ball. She sets up and shoots. *Swish.* Of course. She's Rodriguez.

"Box out!" I hear my dad yell.

Rodriguez receives the ball again and sets up behind the line. Everyone is thinking the same thing: *Will she make it? Or will she bank it?*

She sets up. Right away, I can tell by her form that she's banking it to go for the tie. So, I get into position to box her out. My heart skips.

Head GAMES

Bam. The ball hits the rim and ricochets right back toward Rodriguez's hands. I box Rodriguez out and successfully block her from the rebound. The ball falls into my hands. With Rodriguez tight against me, attempting to foul, I turn around, clasping the ball. Kylie shouts to catch my attention. She's standing in front of me, completely open. I launch the ball toward her. She dribbles and easily lays the ball into our basket.

That's when the buzzer goes off.

sixty-five

The crowd goes nuts. My teammates jump up and down. Our Wildcat mascot tosses blue and yellow confetti into the air. Even the fans join in on the craziness.

After my team releases me from the group huddle, my dad rushes down to the court and smacks me on the back. "Way to go, Spider!" He smiles ear to ear.

I half hug my dad. "Thanks," I say, and I mean it this time.

"Nice job, big sister." My mom embraces me.

When I turn away from my parents, I find myself standing in between Zach and Matt.

"Amazing, Taylor," Zach says. "It's like my playoff game last year when Garrison and I . . ."

I roll my eyes and face Matt, who's beaming.

Zach places his arm around my shoulders.

Instantly, Matt's expression flips.

I wiggle out of Zach's grip. "Listen, I don't want to talk to you. Ever again. I should have never hooked up with you."

Zach opens his mouth to respond and I cut him off, "Seriously, I couldn't care less what you have to say. I don't know if I ever really meant anything to you or not. But I don't care. We're done."

Zach harrumphs, and I turn around to address Matt. "The rehab," I say, out of breath. "And I'm not on your three-B list. . . . And you're not with Violet."

"A what? What are you talking about?"

"And the card. That was so sweet."

Matt looks confused. "Taylor, I never gave you a card."

"You mean you didn't stick a card in my locker the other day and say you wanted to meet me at the beach?" I ask, mentally trying to place the rest of the puzzle pieces together.

That's when Zach taps me on the shoulder and interrupts once more. "Hate to intrude, but I figured I should just break the suspense and let you know that it was me who sent the card. It started out as a three-B thing, but I'd still be into hanging out, especially after seeing how hot you get when you're angry."

I give him a look that screams, "Are you kidding me?!?"

I don't know whether he's totally oblivious or just narcissistic, but he continues, "You sure don't want to meet me at the beach tonight? I'll meet you at eight, just like the card said . . . babe."

"Zach," I reply, "as tempting as that offer is," I roll my eyes, "why don't you just take a hint and leave? Let's just say that: One, my hotness is totally not dependent on whether I'm angry; and two, I can get guys when I want to, and I don't want you."

"Hate to break it to you, *Spider*, but who would think a girl falling off a runway is hot?" Zach rudely retorts.

Matt steps in. "I would."

I give Zach a look, successfully raising one eyebrow (FIRST TIME EVER!!!), and turn to Matt. More butterflies flutter around my stomach than ever before. "You, huh?"

"Yeah . . . me. I've been trying to tell you for a while now, but . . . uh . . . I . . ." Matt fumbles for the right words. And all of a sudden it clicks. The poems: "Chocolate," "Red . . . ." They were about . . . *me*.

I grab Matt's sweatshirt sleeves and, in the middle of the gym, pull Matt's face toward mine, not caring in the slightest if anyone sees. He kisses me gently at first, tasting like cinnamon. Then he pushes harder and deeper. The kiss is amazing and perfect and sparkly and everything I ever imagined a kiss would be. *Wayyyy* better than my kiss with Zach.

When our lips pull apart, I smile and he nuzzles my neck.

"I've been wanting to do that for a long time," Matt whispers in my ear, sending chills down my spine.

Then, I look around and realize that we're standing in the center of the school gymnasium. I hear a few snickers and catcalls, but I decide to ignore them. It was so worth it.

"Taylor!" Coach Jackson calls to me. She's standing next to the SoCal Suns coach. "If you and Mr. Moore have finished whatever business you have together, Coach Delamarte would like to talk to you again."

I let go of Matt's hand and begin walking toward Coach.

However, I'm distracted by the sight of our fans lifting Kylie on their shoulders. "Hey, Taylor!" she shouts. "Come over here."

I look at Coach Delamarte, unsure about what I should do.

"Enjoy your win. The SoCal Suns will definitely be here when you're done," she says.

I mouth "thanks" and jog over to Kylie. When I reach her, I'm promptly hoisted onto some random fan's shoulders in between a flood of people still cheering and chanting Wildcats on the sweaty gym floor . . . all for us. That's when Coach Martie hands Tamika a pair of silver scissors. One by one, Kylie, Tamika, Eva, Missy, Jessica, Zoe, Abby, and I hold the cool heavy scissors and snip down the thick net. Together. As a team. And it's the best feeling in the world.

Finally. I'm going to have the best story to share on Monday morning.

acknowledgements

First off, thank you to Jane Schonberger and everyone at Pretty Tough who work hard everyday to make sure sporty girls are given the respect, acknowledgement, and spotlight they achieve and deserve. It's an honor to write for the Pretty Tough brand. Thank you to Gillian Levinson, Lexa Hillyer, Ben Schrank, and everyone at Razorbill for your hard work. I'm thrilled to work with such an amazing team, especially my Diet Coke–guzzling, hard-working, detail-oriented, and extremely talented editor. A special thank you to my fairy agent, Michelle Grajkowski, for making my dreams come true. I'm truly blessed to have you in my life.

A huge thank-you hug to Christine A. Baker, Lauren Lesser, Stacia Suttles, Katia Raina, Colleen Rowan Kosinski, Carrie Harris, Nicole Destefano, Scott Neumyer, Cyn Balog, Nancy Viau, Michael Troso, and all my sporty buds who read bits and pieces of this book and offered their valuable insight and advice. Also, thanks to Karen Andronici, Sandy Poulton, and Donna Kinn for your career mentorship, guidance, and cheers.

And finally, an enormous thank you to my family. Thanks to my biggest publicists, Mom, Dad, Ron, Ida, and Kelly, for rooting me on, first as an athlete, now as an author. Sydney and Sabrina, thanks for making me giggle and for being my very first audience. Kaci Olivia, thanks for lighting up my life and giving me the courage to write. And last, but certainly not least, thank you Justin, for listening to every single word I type, talking me off the ledge, and for your endless, unyielding support. I love you.

This book was written in memory of Amy Schuenemann Voorhees, a Pretty Tough athlete and teacher, who was taken from this world way too soon.